I0545004

That Summer in Spain

Lawrence I. Hill

Published by Moody Boxfan Books, 2020.

"Goner"

By the Wilted Wallflowers
[from the album, *Shame of the Governess*]

• • • •

I was lost
When I first tasted your lips
My head spun
When my hands gripped your hips
Can't quell the excitement running through my
veins
Baby thanks to you, I'll never be the same

(Cuz I'm a) Goner
Your loving has set me adrift
(Yeah, I'm a) Goner
Craving only your kiss (x2)
Goner, Goner, Baby

Never knew something
Could feel so real
You have me missing love
I never knew I missed
Never wanna return
Even if I'm lost
You've taken me places
I never thought could exist

(And I'm a) Goner

I feel lost at sea
(Oh, I'm a) Goner
Only you can save me (x2)
Goner, Goner, Baby

Oh, it's not like I ever thought I had it all figured out
But seeing your face has me filled with such doubt
I'm questioning all the things I ever knew about me
Yeah, that man's a stranger, oh, who is he

(He's a) Goner
Feeling lost at sea
(And I'm a) Goner
Only you can save me
(Oh just a) Goner
I crave only your sweet kiss
(Cuz I'm a) Goner

This love has thrown me adrift
Goner, Goner, Oh Baby, Goner, Goner
I am just a goner

CHAPTER ONE

D ennis stumbled down the hotel hallway, dragging me with him.

"That was the best wrap party ever!" he yelped.

I laughed and turned toward my room.

"Ah, no, no, no—you're coming with me."

"Dennis, I don't think—"

"GONER!" He began singing in too loud a voice and noticeably off-key. *"Cuz I'm a goner! I feel lost at sea!"*

"Shh!" I hissed. "You'll wake the whole hotel."

But he kept bellowing, so I put my hand over his mouth.

He hummed through my hand and the sensation made me laugh. I moved it away. "The only way you're gonna get me to shut up is if you kiss me."

He pulled me close and kissed me. I made a weak effort to push away.

"Three months in those dusty village rentals," he said, "and now our last couple of nights in this beautiful hotel? I'm taking full advantage."

"I thought you liked our dusty village rentals," I replied.

"I liked that you were across the street, Xavier. That I could see your window at night, and watch until the light clicked off and think about you in bed. Alone. And maybe you were lying there thinking about me too."

He pulled me closer. I wanted to melt into him. Right there, in the hallway of this hotel, leaning against the door. Pull him down to the rough carpet and fold into him.

"Yeah, I'm a goner," he started singing again, but this time in a near whisper. *"Craving only your kiss."*

"Stop singing that song. That's not fair."

"What won't be fair is if you don't spend the night with me." He kissed my neck. "Don't you know how much I want you?"

I looked up at him, with that puppy dog expression on his face. The middle buttons of his shirt had come undone and I slid my hand under the fabric. My fingers played in the soft hair of his chest; I pressed my palm to the heat of his skin.

"It's the last night," he whispered.

"I know," I said, sighing. "That's exactly what I mean. I don't think I can."

He moved his hand from my hip and slowly ran it over my bulging crotch.

"I think you're more than able." He gave a squeeze. "Oh god," he whispered hotly, "you're so hard."

I fell against him, burying my face in his neck, feeling intoxicated all over again.

"And you're an asshole," I whispered.

"Probably."

He gently brought my face in front of his. I felt his hot tongue in my mouth.

"Come inside?" he asked breathlessly.

My body was slack, total surrender.

I could only nod.

• • • •

THE HEAVY DOOR SLAMMED shut behind us. The room was dark except for some light peeking between the slats of the blinds. It made me think of endings, the last reel of a film. Denny reached for the switch.

"No, leave them off," I said.

I went to the window and pulled the cord, bringing the blinds all the way up. Moonlight flooded the small area in front of the window and fell across the room.

"Come here," I said.

Denny walked toward me. Just as he reached the edge of the bed I told him to stop.

"Stay there," I said.

After kicking off my shoes, I tossed my shirt then my pants across the room and let the light fall over my half-naked body. Hooking my thumb in the waistband of my briefs, I pulled one side down slightly, stopping just short of revealing all.

A small gasp escaped Denny's lips and the heat of his stare burned into me.

"You want them off?" I asked.

He nodded.

"Maybe," I shrugged.

"Yes, please," he implored in a throaty whisper. Exhilaration coursed through me.

I ran my fingers along the waistband and then slowly lowered the briefs. They caught on my swollen cock and as I inched the material past, it jumped free with a bounce, jutting out in front of me. I looked Denny in the eyes and he smiled his delicious half-smile.

Naked, I stood there, letting him examine me. My hands played over my freed skin and settled on my cock. Stroking it slowly, I threw my head back and uttered a small moan. A similar sound came from Dennis and he moved toward me.

"Nah," I said, holding up my hand. "No touching. Not yet."

He let out something like a small whimper.

"Now it's your turn."

"My turn?"

"Get undressed," I commanded.

He eagerly complied.

"Slowly," I said.

Struggling against his need, he managed to do as told until he too was in only his underwear. His erection pulled the material taut so that the length of it was outlined. He inched the boxer briefs down at his waist slowly, mimicking me.

"Take them off," I said. "Now."

Biting his bottom lip, he gave me a fierce look.

His long, leanly muscled limbs, thick thighs and round calves, I took it all in. His broad shoulders, his well-defined chest dusted with hair, tapering down over a landscape of lines and angles to his tight waist. His cock stretching up in a pulsing salute.

I moved close to him.

"Tonight, this is all mine."

I ran my hands across his chest, over his abs, around to his hard, round ass, caressing. I pulled his body to mine.

"I thought you said no touching," he said.

I gave him a sudden rough push and he toppled back onto the bed.

He let his arms fall and lay there, chuckling.

"You are in a mood tonight."

"Yep." I climbed on top and straddled him so that our cocks were pressed together. He gave a sharp intake of breath as I began to rock my hips, rubbing us against one another, pinning his arms down and kissing—his mouth, his face, his neck, as much of his body as I could. My lips moved over his nipples, and I buried my face in his pits as he moaned.

"You told me how much you want me?" I said, kissing him.

He nodded.

"Prove it. Show me."

With something like a growl, he grabbed me under the arms and wrestled me onto the bed. He flipped me onto my stomach.

He pressed an arm across my shoulders, pinning me to the mattress, and stroked his dick lightly against my ass. He let it slide slowly, the swollen head rubbing against my hole, teasing me. I bucked against him.

"Fuck me," I commanded.

"Oh yeah?"

"Yes. Hard."

He positioned himself and pressed gently against my opening.

"No," I demanded. "I said fuck me."

With a rough, piercing thrust he at once filled me. I cried out, my back arching.

"Zay?" His voice was heavy with concern.

I ignored his solicitude.

"Don't stop," I said.

He fell on me, grinding his hips, sinking into me as deeply as he could. I felt his fingers in my hair, grabbing the curls. He buried his face in my neck kissing, licking.

He was right. I was in a mood tonight. A mood to forget it all. Not to think of tomorrow morning or yesterday or the last three months. I wanted only this right now. Only this sensation. I wanted to lose myself in this white-hot heat inside me. Only now, only this. I wanted the rest to fade to black.

. . . .

THE RINGTONE FROM MY cell phone felt like someone cracking a slab of wood across my forehead.

I blinked, dazed, foggy-headed, trying to rouse myself. Denny had his arms wrapped tight around me; his deep breathing shuddered against my back, his cock nestled in the cleft of my ass.

He grumbled sleepily as I tried to reach for the phone, pulling me back, grinding his hips against me.

The phone started ringing again, whoever was calling was not giving up. I managed to get an arm free and grab it from the nightstand. It was the production assistant giving me an ETA on when the car would arrive to take me to the airport. And it was soon.

I managed to get out of bed and started searching for my clothes. I pulled on my jeans and ran my hand over my bare chest. I needed a shower but there wasn't time. I would barely be able to dash back to my room and throw everything into a suitcase. I'd have to fly all the way to New York with his dried cum all over my body.

Even when leaving, I'll still be carrying him with me, I thought with a pang. *Leaving.* This was leaving. This wasn't fair. I felt a cold jab in my stomach. Why had I done this to myself? How could I have let it go this far? I knew how it would end all along.

"It's too bad we're not leaving together," Dennis said quietly from the bed.

I snatched up my nearby T-shirt and pulled it on.

"Yeah, well," I said, my voice harder than I intended. "It's probably better this way."

"Hey, Zay, don't—"

He was interrupted by another phone ringing, this time muffled. I rifled through the clothing strewn on the floor and pulled a cell phone from the pocket of his jeans.

The name on the screen read: *Ronnie*

"It's your fiancée," I said, tossing the phone to him roughly.

He caught it, a wounded look in his eyes, and answered.

"Hello? Yeah, hey, babe. Listen, let me call you right back, okay? Yeah, yeah, I'm just in the middle of something. Okay, bye." He hung up as I was heading toward the door. "Xavier?"

I shook my head.

"You're not actually in the middle of something, Denny; you're at the end."

"What's that supposed to mean?"

He sat up, moving to the edge of the bed.

"I've gotta go. My car will be here soon."

"You can't just leave like this."

I turned to him.

"I have to. And you have to go back to being James Dennis, movie star." I waved my hand at the phone in his hand. "Back to your real life."

"My real life?"

"Yes, your real life." I snatched the door open. "Because summer's over."

CHAPTER TWO

T*hree months earlier.*

• • • •

EVERYONE I KNEW HATED airports. Except for me.

I looked around at the bright summer light streaming in all around and closed my eyes at the rush of white noise, letting it soothe me.

Or, at least, I tried to. I had that familiar feeling that could turn this place of escape into a prison. It felt the same as when a flight was grounded, or delayed, or canceled and these great glass walls that I loved when light poured through them suddenly became like a prison—keeping me trapped inside from the world of the living. I wanted it to be my escape, as it usually was, to be my place to chill and hide from the crush as I waited to be carried off to somewhere new and, hopefully, exciting. I wanted it to be my brief spot of Zen. The controlled chaos where I melted away into the great anonymity of masses of people from everywhere in the world; the constant flow of different languages and fashions that disguised me from the ordinary version of myself. I wanted it to be the place where I watched, studied people, gathered the material to create any number of characters from that spot in my mind where all these things got filed away.

But it wasn't—not this time. This time the only thing I felt was the discordant crush of my anxiety. I was a bundle of nerves, and it was spinning me for a loop.

I was headed to Spain for my big break. At least, that's how I thought of it. To everyone else in the industry, this was just a fairly small independent film helmed by a well-respected but foreign filmmaker, Carlos Pedrón. But for me, it was a case of things finally falling into place. I had yearned for so long to sink my teeth into something "real." I'd mostly been doing theater for the last few years, and I loved it, but the film and television projects I'd had come my way were less than challenging, to say the least. It was mainly shallow pretty boy guest spots on TV and a few wise-cracking best friends or co-worker roles on film. The work had gotten me a great agent and some attention in the industry but it was hardly career-making stuff, much less anything that required depths of talent.

I wanted a chance to show what I was made of, to let people know I had real talent. And this was just the project to do that.

So I was already in my head about that and now I was late. The project I'd gotten booked for—some paint-by-numbers romantic comedy where I was, once again, the quippy sweater-wearing sensible best friend—had run well over its shooting schedule. I was supposed to have been in La Mancha over a week prior, but I was only just now getting out of New York. The rest of the crew and cast had been in Spain for almost two weeks, getting to know each other, building relationships, and even getting started on the work—rehearsals, if nothing else. And here I was, making a fashionably late entrance, the dumb, inexperienced kid who thought he was too good to show up with everybody else. At least, that's what I worried they were thinking of me. Filmmaking, especially indie filmmaking, is something like trench warfare—and if I wasn't in the trenches with the rest of my comrades, I was worried they wouldn't trust me as readily.

And then—it was hard to even admit it to myself—there was another stumbling block. Perhaps the biggest, at least the tallest.

James Dennis Herbert.

My co-star.

The golden-skinned Adonis with the piercing. The Hollywood heartthrob, the box office draw, the Quintessential Leading Man. And the star I'd idolized—had crushed on—ever since middle school. He was only four years older than me but he had been acting since he was a teenager. I could distinctly remember twelve-year-old Xavier, struggling with his budding sexuality and unsure of himself, sitting in the movie theater with his friends. It was a dumb movie, make no mistake, called *Tidal Wave*—about a group of teenage surfers who solve the mystery surrounding a rash of local murders. And there he was, rising out of the water, glistening and shining like some sort of sun god, carrying a boogie board and wearing nothing but his swim trunks. When he lifted his arm to brush the wet hair from his eyes, I was suddenly no longer struggling with my sexuality. I knew then exactly what I was interested in. The only discomfort I felt was trying to position my extra-large soda in my lap so that it disguised my swelling surety.

From then on I followed his career like some starry-eyed groupie. First, it was just because he was my fantasy, my dream guy, my movie star crush. But as I got older, moving through high school, and my hobbies solidified into aspirations and goals and I realized that I wanted to become an actor, he became a role model. As he too got older and out of his teens, he found work that allowed him to showcase his abilities. He was still gorgeous, of course, and made all the appropriate listicles for Hot Guys, but his work choices changed. He got real roles in real films and became a legitimate movie star.

And, somehow, he managed to remain humble and cool. Or, at least, that's how he came across in interviews and press. I admired that and wanted it for myself. I wanted to be a mover in the industry but not give in to all the pomp and circumstance that kept some stars floating way above the ground, ridiculous in their lack of self-awareness and out of touch.

Now I was finally getting to meet my former crush—and, not only that but act with him in a film. It was hard to wrap my mind around. What really set my head spinning the most, though, was the fact that I was going to be playing his romantic interest. I was going to be on-screen playing James Dennis Herbert's lover. What the entire fuck?

When the film was offered to me the co-lead hadn't been cast. I didn't care, of course, because it was an amazing script and an opportunity I would have killed for. I never would have guessed that they would end up casting James Dennis. He epitomized the masculine heartthrob: part action star, part romantic heartbreaker, and no parts artsy gay character. It floored me. And then the anxiety set in.

I had nothing to hide for myself, I'd come out publicly pretty early in my career. But I'd had some really weird moments with male co-stars in the past. A lot of the usual machismo bullshit and paranoia on their part—not wanting to interact with me too much outside of the scene, making sure we weren't seen together in public, even at the press junkets—it was sometimes really uncomfortable. No matter how liberal they claimed they were, straight guys had serious fucking issues. At least, that was my experience.

I couldn't let that get in my way, though, when I read this script. I had to be in this film. But who knew I would end up having to get down and dirty with the guy I'd been fantasizing about for half of my life. Now I was the one with serious, fucking issues. What if I acted like a fangirl and completely embarrassed myself? What if I got a little too into the more intimate scenes and revealed myself, so to speak? It could be pretty hard to feel too sexy in a scene with a crew standing around watching and a lighting rig highlighting every flaw. But this wasn't just some random scene partner—this was the sun god himself.

My cell rang and I jolted up in my waiting lounge seat, shaken from the cloud of anxiety fogging my mind.

"Bitch!" a voice rang out from the VidChat app. "Where have you been?"

It was my best friend Jaelyn. She and I first met doing a play together on Broadway when we were both nineteen. It was a coming-of-age story that had our characters falling in love. We got on like a house on fire, and despite popular notions to the contrary, it translated to insane chemistry onstage. We got rave reviews and it gave both of our careers the kick-starts they needed. We'd been as close as siblings ever since, even though now her career kept her on the West Coast most of the year. Thanks to her amazing singing voice, she'd landed as a lead on a show about a high school full of non-stop singing and dancing.

"I've been trying to reach you for days," she added with loving censure.

"I just wrapped last night and I had to get some sleep before my flight."

"Oh wow! Off to Spain immediately?"

"Oh yeah. I've barely had time to catch my breath but I'm already behind schedule."

She chewed her lip. "So I guess you didn't hear the news?"

"What news? You know I'm on a social media diet when I'm shooting. What happened?"

"Max."

My heart skipped a beat.

"Max? What happened? Is he all right?"

Jaelyn grimaced and tilted her head.

"Oh yeah, he's definitely all right." She sighed. "He's great, in fact."

"I mean, I'm happy for him. I guess? But you didn't really call me just to tell me that my asshole ex is doing great, did you?"

"I don't know how you ever dated somebody named Maxim, anyway. It's the worst."

I rolled my eyes.

"It's a family name—which you already know. Anyway, stop avoiding the subject."

"You know he's been dating Matthew Keene."

"Of course," I said.

"Well, they went to this premiere last week. Together. And this reporter from *Evening Stars* made note of it. So basically Max told them that he and Matthew were a couple. The next morning he confirmed it on social media, and, basically, he's officially out."

"You've gotta be fucking kidding me."

"Sorry, babe."

I had a bitter taste in my mouth and shook my head, trying to stave off the anger.

"All that drama. For three years," I said. "And then out of nowhere, he dumps me. He said he wasn't comfortable with people knowing about him. He had his 'career to consider' blah blah blah."

I broke off, remembering the hurt. I had been absolutely stunned and heartbroken. It had only been within the last few months when I'd finally realized I had moved past it.

"It hasn't even been eighteen months yet," I continued. "And he's already proclaiming to the world that he's gay? It sure didn't take long for him to change his mind."

Jaelyn gave me a comforting look.

"I know, babe, and I'm sorry. I didn't mean to make you upset. But I wanted to let you know before anyone got to you. I didn't want them springing this on you *TMZ*-style or something."

I nodded. "Thank you," I muttered.

"But, whatever, fuck him," Jaelyn declared. "You've got a kick-ass project lined up. And you're on your way to spend the summer in Spain. All that wine and all those hot men! You're better off without that punk anyway."

"I guess." I shrugged.

"No, baby, you know. And you know I love you. I mean, do you really need more than that?"

I couldn't help but smile.

"I guess not," I said, forcing a cheeriness I didn't exactly feel. "Thank you for letting me know, for real. But I better go, they're going to be calling my gate soon."

"Okay, babe. Call me when you're settled in. Unless one of those hot Spanish men gets you first. Love you."

"Love you, too."

"And remember if anybody has something to say about Maximus Asshole and his boy toy, don't even sweat it. That's his problem now."

I blew her a kiss and hung up. But, despite the pep talk, I couldn't help but wonder if the problem was me.

CHAPTER THREE

About eleven hours later, Max and heartbreak were the last things on my mind. The flight from JFK had sat on the runway for longer than I cared to remember, and once I'd finally landed in Madrid, the train I was scheduled to take had left without me. So I struggled with my luggage onto the platform and waited, miserable and sweating. I hadn't been prepared for the heat. It was summer, obviously, and I had been told that this area of the country was warm, but it hit me like being tossed into a desert without warning. I tried to calm down and remember that I would have time to make myself presentable once I got to La Mancha.

The train ride, at least, gave me a chance to concentrate on something besides my nerves. As we rolled into Castille-La Mancha, I grinned at the sight of a line of windmills. It was just like out of the stories, and I could see Don Quixote, lance at his side, galloping toward the giant monsters that threatened him. But, I wondered, what if it was a sign? What if I was the delusional nobleman who thought he'd been granted a higher purpose when I was really just on the path to destruction and humiliation? I shook my head and tried to ignore those ever-present doubts. This was my shot, I couldn't sabotage it before it had begun.

I was tripping over myself, dragging my luggage behind me and trying to respond to a dozen texts I'd missed during transit as I stumbled into the hotel lobby where I was supposed to be meeting the cast and crew. My mind was racing, and I kept chastising myself silently to chill the fuck out. But as soon as I caught sight of him across the lobby, I came to a halt, captivated.

My eyes wouldn't leave him. As he stood talking with Carlos Pedrón, the director, it seemed as if there was some glow around him, a golden aura like he had been backlit—as if he was playing a mystical being in a fantasy story. James Dennis Herbert. The sun god himself. Light, energy, joy just seemed to pulse around him, emanating out and touching everyone and everything nearby. When Dennis smiled, even my most gloomy mood stood little chance against the radiance. And when sadness clouded his beautiful face it never failed to break my heart. This I would come to soon learn, all too well.

"Ah, there he is," said Carlos, catching sight of me.

He turned to look at me, following Carlos's nod, and he seemed to light up even more.

My stomach did a dozen flips and I felt suddenly too small for my own body. So this was what it felt like to have James Dennis Herbert, movie star, hold me in his gaze. It felt as if I'd just walked on stage, my first cue, and the spotlight was hitting me. My skin tingled.

"Xavier!" he cried and rushed toward me.

I nervously tucked a fallen curl behind my ear and extended my hand for a shake but he brushed it aside and wrapped his arms around me. I'm six-one myself and not used to feeling slight, but he towered over me by several inches. I felt his large hands on my back as we hugged and I swore if he had reared back just a bit he would have lifted me off the floor. This dude was massive.

"Buddy, so good to finally meet you!" His deep voice rumbled against my neck and sent a small shiver down me.

"Carlos has told me so much about you, I've really been looking forward to this."

"Me too, James, nice to meet you. I'm such an admirer of your work—"

"Nope, nope," he interrupted. "You have to call me Dennis, Denny—all my friends do—or at least Jim. But no James—that's my dad—and please, *please* no Jimmy—that's me when I was twelve and it was scary enough the first time. Oh, and no "admirer of your work" bullshit either. No jerking each other off—we'll save that for later."

He winked and my mouth fell open slightly. He chuckled.

"I'm sorry, bad joke. But I want us to be comfortable around each other. Deal?"

"Sure thing, Jimmy." I teased.

"Oh, my man has jokes, huh?" He cackled and tried to grab me in a neck hold but I dodged out of the way, laughing.

He was about to give chase when Carlos stepped in, waving his hands.

"Boys, boys. Save this energy for the set, yes? We still have to meet with the investors from São Paulo before we head to location. We don't want you showing up with the broken limbs, no?"

"More investors?" asked Denny, with a slight grimace. "Is the funding still up in the air?"

"It's fine, it's fine," said Carlos. "*No te preocupes, mi amor.* This is what happens when you make the independent film, no? They just want to meet you and make sure their money is well spent. And how can they resist these faces?"

"I always say the wrong thing. It'd probably be best if I just shut up and look pretty," said Denny.

"Yes, this is probably true," answered Carlos in a deadly serious tone.

Dennis burst out laughing and Carlos joined in. I was relieved at the easy camaraderie we all seemed to share. I knew then that this was going to be a special project. But I could never have dreamt exactly how special.

• • • •

WE WERE HEADED FOR a small village in the heart of La Mancha where Carlos had grown up. Carlo told us that he wanted to come back to this place to make his film because it was special. The building we would be filming in was a villa of sorts. It had once been a hotel decades ago, a sort of boutique hotel, almost like a resort, for the elite of the Franco era. Then it had been bought and turned into a private residence. Now, through movie magic, we were taking it over and teasing out the ghosts to bring it back into its former life as a hotel. The villa was about an hour's drive from the city. Some of the crew had gone ahead on the train and the rest of us would be following with the costumes and equipment by car and truck. I was surprised Dennis hadn't taken the more comfortable train option but Carlos said he insisted on hanging back until I showed up so he could meet me. I tried to hide my sudden goofy smile when he told me this.

I knew very little of La Mancha and only just a little more Spanish than that. Besides asking for a *café* or where the *baño* was, my rudimentary two years of high school language had left me with very little.

I was not prepared for the overwhelming beauty. Golden landscapes stretching far and wide, the sun shimmering just above the surface. Some areas appeared desolate, stark in their beauty. And then suddenly we would come down the other side of a hill and there would be vineyards stretching on either side of us, long bursts of small green bushes tied to lines, with glorious mountains in the distance. We even passed windmills, like great gods out of the myths, and it all felt like a storybook.

I wondered, gazing at the vast spaces around us, what it would be like to make a film so far away from... well, everything. I could tell Denny had similar thoughts on his mind as he stared at the landscape wide-eyed.

We were sharing an SUV with two of the crew up front. It was a long drive and they rambled on to one another in Spanish. I didn't want the silence to get awkward, although Denny seemed anything but uncomfortable. Still, I worked up the nerve to strike up a conversation.

"Can I ask you something?" I said once we had gotten past all the usual small talk.

"Shoot. Ask me anything."

"Why are you doing this film?"

Dennis cocked his head and he suddenly looked guarded. I was sure I had offended him.

"Sorry, that didn't come out right. What I mean is—look, I'm barely out of drama school. I've got a couple of credits to my name. So even though this is tiny and there's no budget, when Carlos Pedrón calls, it's a no-brainer. But you, you're like a genuine fucking movie star."

Dennis gave me a small smile and the guard dropped a little. He shook his head.

"It's the same for me, man. I mean, sure, the pay's not much. But it's Carlos-fucking-Pedrón. Hell yeah, I'm going to do it.

And 'movie star' is maybe a step too far. I'm like ten minutes and a kung fu grip away from being a cartoon character."

"What? You're crazy, man. You're a fucking awesome actor."

I was interrupted by a chastising lift of the brow.

I smiled. "No, seriously. I'm for real. I'm not just jerking you off."

"Not yet," he said with another cheeky wink.

I shoved him in mock disgust. "Shut up, you know what I mean. Like, you're a for-real actor. And this—well, this is kinda risky."

He waved away my concern.

"I've heard all that, a dozen times and more, from my agent and anybody else who I told about this. And that's exactly why I'm doing it. I'm tired of all that cops and robbers shit. If I have to do one more stunt scene, I'll lose it. I mean, don't get me wrong, it's a lot of fun. And I've been lucky. That stuff paid well. Maybe nobody took me seriously as an actor but I had fun. And I learned a lot. But I'm getting older and I need more."

"Older? You're not even thirty yet. Come on."

"I know, but I've been doing this since I was a kid. And it's just time for... something else. It's like my first big movie—after I got off of that TV show—I keep thinking about it."

"*Call Waiting*? That was great."

"No, not that one. Before that, it was this small drama where I played the troubled younger brother of the main character—*My Parents*. Nobody saw it, but I loved doing it. It felt like there was a point, you know, like what I was doing had something to say. And it did zilch at the box office but the director of *Call Waiting* saw it and that's what got me in there. So it felt like this huge blessing." He shook his head and laughed at his introspection. "And then it was all downhill from there. A washed-up action star at twenty-eight."

"'Washed-up,' yeah right. I'll be so lucky to be washed-up by your age."

"My age?" He punched me playfully in the shoulder.

"So you're not worried about alienating your fan base, then?"

"Dude. You sound like one of those YouTubers. 'Your fan base.' You've got all the jargon."

"You know what I mean. You don't think your action movie audience will be kinda thrown by a movie in a small, sleepy Spanish village where two dudes fall in love?"

He turned away from me and looked out of the window at the passing fields.

"Yeah, of course," he said after a moment. "I mean, some of them will." He shrugged. "But, hey, fuck 'em, right? It's just a movie, you know."

I nodded.

"And what about you, Mister Intrepid Reporter? Aren't you worried about alienating your fan base?"

"My fan base? You mean my mom and my grandma? Nah, I think they'll be cool with it. They're just glad I've got a paying gig."

"Amen to that."

"Besides," I hesitated, unsure if I should go there yet. But he did say we should be comfortable so better now than later. "Besides, I came out a few years ago."

"Oh?"

"Yeah, during the press junket for this film I was doing. There were these rumors about me and my co-star and I didn't want to evade any of the questions anyway, so I just decided to do it. I told the next reporter who asked that I'm gay. It clearly didn't make a lot of headlines or anything, but I don't think anyone who knows about me will be surprised by this film choice."

"Wow, that's brave, man."

I shrugged. "It's just what it is, you know. It's not brave, it's just the truth."

Denny blinked. "Yeah, I guess so." He looked out of the window again.

I gritted my teeth and tried to calm my sudden anxiety.

"That's gonna be cool, right?" I asked nervously.

"What?" He turned back, bemused.

"That's not gonna make it weird or anything."

"Weird?"

"Yeah, there are some pretty graphic scenes in the script. And I mean, you know, I know you're not—well, I just mean, I don't want you to be uncomfortable if you think, like, maybe I'm attracted to you— N-n-not that I am, I'm just saying." Fuck, what was wrong with me? If I could punch my own mouth shut I would have. "I just mean, I don't want you to feel weird or uncomfortable or anything just because—"

He put his hand on my knee to stop my prattle and it worked.

"Dude, chill. It's completely fine. It's a movie. I've had to kiss plenty of people on-screen. You can't let all that other shit get into it. If you're attracted to them, them to you, whatever, it's all secondary to the work."

I nodded. "Of course. Sorry."

He patted my knee, which somehow made me feel all the more mortified. "Don't worry, buddy. Hell, Ronnie probably loves it."

"Ronnie?"

"My fiancée. I think she's getting a kick out of me playing gay. In fact, I think she wants to see this film more than anybody. She says it's gonna be hot." He punched me playfully in the shoulder again. "So we can't disappoint her, right?"

He gave me one of his big, beaming smiles and I couldn't do anything but smile back.

"Right. Can't disappoint Ronnie," I said with a forced chuckle.

As I turned to look out of the window myself, all I could think about was my knee. My skin still seemed to pulse with heat from where his touch had lingered. If just him patting me on the knee had done that to me, what were those sex scenes gonna be like? My body stirred at the mere thought.

I chewed on my bottom lip and tried to concentrate on the scenery going by.

Fuck, I thought. *This is going to be a long shoot.*

CHAPTER FOUR

The first weeks of shooting, in fact, seemed particularly designed to make me a mental case. Here I was portraying this guy who is conflicted about his burgeoning sexuality and falls, head over heels, for another guy who he assumes to be straight. Not only does he assume him to be straight but he knows him by reputation to be a ladies' man. Because of that, he tries and tries to deny his more than obvious feelings, and then when he does finally admit them, he struggles to not let them be known.

The film was loosely based on an episode in Carlos's youth. Before he became a filmmaker, he'd worked at a local hotel and during one fateful summer, in which he was only just admitting to himself who he really was, he fell in love with a visiting American tourist. The true story didn't end so well, with Carlos being left heartbroken as the American returned home, his dalliance with Carlos a forgotten experiment. But Pedrón had decided to re-write history with his film and not only would the visiting American return the young hotel worker's affections; he himself would fall madly in love too.

This film meant a lot to our director, not only because it was based on his own experience but because he had chosen to re-write the outcome, to reclaim his own history in a way, and give his younger self the happy ending he'd never had. It was his most highly personal film to date—and possibly his riskiest. He had never shied away from gay themes or characters in his work, but he had made a name for himself doing surrealist comedies and political satire. He had come of age in a directly

Post-Franco Spain and it informed much of his early work. The world saw Carlos Pedrón as a social commentator, a humorous critic, not as a teller of romance stories. And despite our supposed advances in social acceptance, there still weren't a lot of happily-ever-afters for gay characters on the movie screen. So the studios were scared to touch it. They wanted the product that they had always known, a sure thing, a guaranteed box office. But Carlos stuck to his guns.

As a result, he was forced to find all the financing himself. The money was coming from dozens of places all over the world. Enter the investors from São Paulo, who despite seeming to enjoy our meeting, took two weeks to confirm their involvement. Two long weeks where we had begun to shoot, unsure if we could even finish the film. Two weeks until the biggest chunk of our money was guaranteed.

Add to that—me. When I was deep in the work, I would lose myself. It felt like a cliché. I had always heard stories of actors falling for their co-stars and dismissed it as an excuse, just an anecdote that sounds good for the behind-the-scenes gossip. But it had happened to me before. When I was in a moment and digging deep inside myself to convince whoever was watching, the audience, the critics, whoever, that my scene partner was the love of my life, I'd convinced myself. And I'd learned that it was part of the process. In some small way, I have always fallen in love with my co-stars, the whole company, even the crew, somehow. I had to create an interior world in which *I* believed in order to make it a believable performance.

But I always managed to mentally disconnect when it was finished. I never struggled to return to the real world, to reality. With Dennis, it felt as if there was no disconnect. I would do a scene with the actress playing my aunt, and then afterward, we would chat at lunch like old school friends, no trace of the fictional relationship interfering. But it wasn't the same with Dennis. There was always the specter of something, even when we finished a rehearsal or a scene, that lingered and never fully dispersed. I tried to brush it off as nothing. I told myself it was just a residual effect of my longtime crush. I convinced myself that it was just because I had idolized him for all these years, and now I was finally getting to make believe, in real-time, that I was in love with him.

But even as I told myself that over and over, I knew something was different this time. This wasn't just a crush.

I knew something was definitely different this time because, for all the rush of things I was thinking and feeling, I didn't mention any of it to Jaelyn. We told each other everything but with Dennis, I hardly shared a thing. I sent her a picture of the two of us on set early in the shoot and when she replied, *"OMG he's sooooo hot!"* all I did was reply with a smiley. How could I admit to her that in two short weeks I actually thought I was falling for this guy? This guy, this Hollywood star, this action hero with a beautiful model girlfriend—no, sorry—beautiful model *fiancée*. It was dumb, it was destructive, it was headed down a dead-end. And it was all I could think about.

"No, no, *amor*, I do not rehearse," declared Carlos on our first day on set.

"Wait, like not at all?" asked Dennis.

"No, of course not. I want every moment to be honest, to be true. And rehearsing kills the truth. To me, I am always looking for the truth."

Denny gave me a wide-eyed look. "And we're shooting this on film, right?" he asked Carlos.

"*Pues, claro*. I do not shoot on digital. *Nunca; jamas.*"

"So how many takes do we get?"

"As many as you need, *mi amor*. But you will not need many, of this I'm sure. You are both amazing actors—that is why I cast you—and I trust you. If I trust you, you will be good. *Bueno, es simple.*"

Denny turned to me and whispered, "So we're rehearsing at your place tonight then, right?"

"*Pues, claro, mi amor*," I said in my best Carlos impression.

Denny let out a bark of laughter and punched me in the shoulder. "Awesome, it's a date, buddy."

That was how the torture began, with a simple invitation to rehearse together.

Besides a scant few crew members, who either spoke no English or seemingly had no interest in corny American actors, we were the only people around our age. And with our limited Spanish, it was just easy to stick together. We shot mostly during the day for the first few weeks, so we had the nights and days off to ourselves. We became constant companions. When we weren't working on our scenes together, we were listening to music or watching movies or checking out a local restaurant or swimming, or whatever we decided to do. But always together, just the two of us. Once the funding was finally secure, everyone else seemed to be more at ease, their anxiety seemed to fade. Conversely, mine ratcheted up. I loved spending so much time with Dennis, but it was a challenge to remember that we were only friends, professional colleagues as well, and nothing more.

Dennis had found a buddy, someone to pass the time with and pal around. But, for me, it was different. And I never wanted him to be uncomfortable or keep his distance because of how I felt about him. I didn't want to let on in case it freaked him out. So I tried to be cool, but, admittedly, being cool had never come easy to me.

• • • •

THE VIRGIN MARY LOOMED before me, vibrantly colored and gilded around her edges. The church had looked unprepossessing from the outside—faded brick, straight, plain lines, a solitary bell tower with no remarkable features. But inside the place was magnificent. Vaulted ceilings, ornamentation all around, and, at the front, a grand marvel of an altar. Intricately beautiful frescoes, statuary, and sculpted icons in bronze and gold and silver.

It was another one of our day trips outside the village. Those trips that Dennis insisted on. Just the two of us, alone, exploring as far as we could.

The church was cool and drenched in shadows. It had felt like a breath of fresh air when we first discovered it. The sunlight here was like something I had never experienced, intense and unbroken. It was heat and blinding light, yes, but it was almost transformative. Everything was so stark; the sky, cloudless most of the time, a punch of blue and the fields stretching on and on, blending away so that they seemed never to end. We had passed a field of sunflowers on our hike here, and they seemed like an ocean of gold to me. Little black eyes peering out only occasionally when the rare, weak breezes passed. Standing there, looking out over them, Dennis seemed like some sort of king, his sun-kissed skin reflecting their golden shine.

I felt hands on my shoulders from behind.

Dennis leaned in and spoke quietly.

"That big cabinet thing is amazing."

The feel of his breath on my neck, his voice in this quiet space, sent a tremor through me. I tried to distract myself by spouting some facts.

"It's called a *retablo*—it's Baroque in style."

His hands remained on me, and now he moved them, in soft glides, massaging my shoulders and neck. I wanted to shrug him off, the feeling was driving me crazy, but I didn't want to seem weird. Still, I had to control my breathing as I felt my cock jump to life, emboldened by his closeness. I quickly folded my hands in front of my lap, attempting to shield it from view.

"A what?" he asked.

"A *retablo*," I repeated. I cleared my throat. "It's carved entirely from wood."

"How do you know that?" he asked with a soft chuckle. "You're amazing."

"Oh, nah," I said smiling. "I just grabbed one of the pamphlets by the front door."

I held it up to show him, trying to ignore the situation below my belt. He gave my shoulders one final squeeze.

"Well, this is going on Instagram," he said, pulling out his phone. He stepped back, framing his shot, and I stepped aside.

"Nu-uh," he said. "Get back in there."

"Oh, no," I protested. "You don't want me in your picture."

I stood at an angle to him so my only slightly subsided erection wasn't obvious.

"No, get back to where you were," he commanded playfully. "You don't have to smile or anything. Just stand there, like you were doing, looking up at the *reblato*, or whatever it's called."

I laughed at his mangled Spanish but conceded, glad to be facing away from the camera.

"Perfect," he said when he'd gotten the shot. "I'm gonna tag you. What's your handle?"

I felt my cell vibrate in my pocket alerting me to his tag and follow request. I followed him back and looked at the picture. I was there, in front of the resplendent Mary, in silhouette. It was actually a pretty poetic shot, and I felt a stirring of emotions.

"There are hardly any pictures in your feed," he said, scrolling on his phone.

"What do you mean? I post all the time."

"Yeah, you have beautiful shots. But there are hardly any pictures *of you*—not enough Xavier."

I shrugged. "Ah, I'm not big on selfies. Who wants to look at me anyway?"

"Really, dude? Come off it. If I had a face like yours I'd be constantly snapping selfies."

My stomach did flips. Was he doing this on purpose, or was it just my crazy emotions—and hormones, obviously—making it seem so?

"What in the world are you talking about?" I protested. "Man, you're like the epitome of handsome. Haven't you been on the sexiest bachelors list like half a dozen times?"

He rolled his eyes.

"That's just PR team bullshit at work—that stuff's not real. Anyone with a decent publicist can get on one of those dumb lists."

"I'm not buying it," I teased. "It's not all hype. I've seen you in person, that ain't no Photoshop."

He gave me a crooked half-smile.

"Oh yeah? So it's not so bad in real life, huh?"

I suddenly wanted to hide my face. A little ripple of what felt like laughter ran through me. My dick stirred again. What was wrong with me?

"I mean... you're all right," I joked.

He chuckled, tilting his head back and giving me a once over. *Oh god*, I thought, *please don't let him notice.*

"You're all right too, buddy," he said.

We looked at each other.

"Now, come on," he said, slapping my shoulder. "The Head of Catering told me there's a terrific bakery near here. They apparently have these amazing marzipan cookies. I'm buying."

• • • •

THE BUS HIT A BUMP in the road and shook me awake. I had dozed off not long after we'd left the sleepy little village with the church. I couldn't tell how long I'd been asleep but the sun was starting to set. I turned my head to face Dennis who was beside me. He had his elbow propped on the glass and his chin resting in his palm as he stared outside, watching the landscape go by. Aside from the bright colors in the sky, there wasn't much to look at, yet he seemed to be studying something intently. I could just make out his reflection in the half-darkened window and I saw his eyes were cast down. He was lost in thought.

Our eyes met in the reflection. I felt embarrassed for staring and quickly turned my head. A second later I felt him bump his shoulder against mine. Meeting his gaze I saw that he was smiling warmly.

"Hey sleepyhead, have a good nap?" he asked.

"Was I out for long?"

"Not too long," he said, cutting his eyes at me. "But that must have been some dream you were having?"

"What?" I asked, suddenly stricken. I knew I had a tendency to talk in my sleep. What if I had been dreaming about him? But, of course, I had been dreaming about him—I always seemed to be lately. I braced myself. "Was I talking in my sleep? What did I say?"

He smiled his wicked half-smile.

"I couldn't really make out much, it was mostly mumbling," he said. "And a few little moans."

I felt the color drain from my face.

"Oh god," I muttered and hung my head.

He laughed. "Don't worry, buddy. It wasn't anything. I could just hear you because you were so close to me."

He bumped his shoulder against mine again.

"Hey, don't sweat it." He reached over and lightly lifted my chin. "I'm just giving you a hard time—it was nothing."

I looked at him sheepishly, and he winked at me.

"Everything's okay, buddy."

I let out a soft chuckle and nodded.

"Much longer 'til we get there?" I asked.

He shrugged, rolling his eyes. "Well, they claim it's an hour but at the rate the driver is going, who knows." He rested his arm on mine. "Why, you in a rush to get back?"

"Oh, no, no," I said quickly. "Just wondering."

"It's nice, right?" he said. "All this quiet. The world seems so calm out here."

I nodded.

"What were you thinking about?" I asked hesitantly. "Just now, looking out the window, you seemed lost in thought."

"Oh, I dunno." He looked back out at the, now dark, terrain. "I guess I was just thinking about everything."

"Everything?"

He shrugged. "The film, it got me thinking. Just how it's about Carlos when he was younger, and the things he told us about that time in his life. He had some hard knocks, of course, and some heartbreak, but he just seems to have had so much figured out even then. About who he was and, just, everything."

"And you didn't?"

"Me?" He scoffed. "No, I was a mess at that age."

"You were already a movie star at that age."

He shook his head. "I was an actor, but hardly a movie star. And, regardless, I was a mess."

"It sure didn't look that way. You always looked great and seemed so pulled-together in interviews and stuff. You didn't seem like a typical teen at all."

He looked at me. "Well, maybe I'm a better actor than I think."

"No." I shook my head and then realized. He laughed.

"I mean, yes, yes," I stuttered. "You are an amazing actor. I just mean that you always seem to know just what to say and you were so grounded. It was genuine, not studied. You seemed so real, like someone you would want to be friends with—not like some cool kid who you wanna know because they're popular. But somebody who draws you in because you can just feel their warmth, their magnetism."

I realized he was staring at me and that I had been rambling.

"I mean..." I nervously tucked a curl behind my ear. "That's what I thought at least. You know, from like... TV or whatever."

The corner of his mouth turned up.

"Seems like you were paying attention."

I dropped my eyes.

"Yeah, I guess so."

He hunkered down in his seat so that we were at the same height and leaned against me.

"I'm really flattered you thought you saw all of that in me. But that's not at all how I felt. I was so... just scared and confused." He chewed on his thumbnail. "The year before I got my first big role, I'd had this major growth spurt, right? But before that, I was this chubby, weird, little kid with braces. I had even tried out for the same producers like two years before my first movie and they told me I was never going to get work except for the fat funny kid. They suggested I hire a personal trainer and get a retainer. A personal trainer, man! At twelve years old. But then puberty hit hard—I'm talking Mack truck into a brick wall hard—and suddenly, boom, I'm this tall and lanky creature. But people started to pay attention. And once I got the metal off my teeth, I started getting auditions and callbacks. And, of course, it was great. I'm really lucky and I know it. But at the time, I was floundering—it was all just the massive whirlpool in my head and I couldn't get a grip."

"So what happened?"

"Veronica." He sighed. "We met on a job, and she was the same age as me but she had been modeling since she was a little kid. So she knew all the ropes—she was like a little adult. And for whatever reason, she took to me and protected me. Don't get me wrong, my mom was a great mom. But when the work started coming, and success happened, she didn't really have any reference points for that world. Ronnie guided me, and she and her mom helped me and my mom navigate it all. We became really close."

I felt a twinge in my chest. I couldn't tell if it was the empathy I felt for the picture he painted of the lost little boy or the jealousy I felt knowing that Ronnie was so special to him.

"So you guys are like high school sweethearts then," I said.

Our eyes met and he stared at me for a second. There was something in his expression I couldn't decipher. I wanted to ask him something else, but I didn't know what, and the hesitation felt mutual.

"Eventually," he finally said. He glanced away, cracking his knuckles. "First, it was just like brother and sister. At least, that's how I felt. Then eventually I realized I must be in love with her, and she seemed to agree. Everybody loved it, of course. The agents, the studio—hell, even our parents. It was the perfect story—the two wide-eyed kids who met in Hollywood and fell in love. You couldn't write a better script. And it was great, definitely. I felt so safe and attached to reality when I was with her. I'm sure having her saved my life."

I nodded slowly.

"Well, you're both thriving now so it looks like it was as great as everyone thought."

"I guess," he said softly, peering out of the window. "I owe her so much. And I truly do love her. But, sometimes, I just wonder."

He sounded so sad just then. I wanted to pull him close and wrap my arms around him. But I settled for just leaning into his shoulder.

"'Wonder'? About?"

He was silent for a moment before replying.

"Sometimes I just wonder what if I hadn't figured it out. What if I had gone off the rails—or made a mess of it, or whatever. It wouldn't have been so clean and neat, and maybe I wouldn't have the career I have now. But maybe I would be..."

"Maybe you would be?"

"I don't know. Maybe I would be different. Sometimes I feel like my whole career—my whole life even—has been this image. It's a great image, and people love it. But sometimes I feel like maybe I got lost in there somewhere—the real me, I mean—and I started believing the image was me just like everybody else. And I'm not even sure I know who the real me ever was, or who he is now."

He paused and I waited for him to continue.

"Sorry," he said. "I didn't mean to dump all that on you. This was supposed to be a chill, relaxing escape."

"No, don't apologize," I insisted. "I like that you shared that with me. And, for what it's worth, you seem pretty real to me. I don't think you lost yourself at all."

He continued to look out of the window but he leaned back so that his head rested on my shoulder. I could smell his hair, the salty and sweet tang of his body.

"That's because it's easy with you," he said quietly. "It's different. You're different. I don't feel like I have to turn anything on when I'm around you—no special effects needed. I can just be plain old me."

"You can."

It felt like a paltry response, inadequate. But I didn't know what else to say. I felt that if I said more then I would say too much, and I wasn't sure I would have the ability to stop the flood of whatever came once it was released. So I said nothing more.

I let my cheek rest against his head, breathing deeply of him, and we rode the rest of the way in blissful silence.

CHAPTER FIVE

"**I**'m not sure I'm up for this," Dennis proclaimed.

I took another sip of wine and placed the glass beside me on the floor.

"Yeah," I said, "these sex scenes are kind of intimidating."

He chuckled. "That's not what I was referring to."

"Oh no?" I said, suddenly a bit embarrassed for having revealed my own anxiety.

We were sitting on the floor of my flat, with all of the windows open, in shorts and T-shirts, hoping for a breeze. Summer, in its heat, was pushing in on us and even the nights were getting to be overwhelming.

"No, actually I mean the emotional stuff," he said.

Dennis fanned himself with the script and stretched out his legs—his long, muscular, sun-kissed legs—letting one rest against mine.

"I mean, sure, it's intimidating to get naked in front of a whole bunch of strangers. But I've been pretty close to that in a lot of my other projects. No, what scares me is having to be so... well, so vulnerable on-screen. To open up like that for the whole world to see how sensitive you can be—it's fucking frightening."

"But you're one of the most open people I know."

"I'm friendly, sure. But this guy, this character, I've never had to be him before. He's like a real person—complicated. He's an asshole one minute and then the next he's the most affable dude you know. I don't know if I have the depth."

I scoffed.

41

"Of course you do. Just because you've never been given the chance, doesn't mean you don't have the ability. I know you don't like me to talk about it, but I've seen your films, you're great. No, you haven't had to be this kind of guy but it's in there, you can see the layers in every choice you make. You're not just some walking mannequin, spouting lines, you have real talent."

Dennis shook his head.

"Thank you," he said. "Seriously. Thank you for listening to my bullshit and therapizing me. And thank you for the encouragement. You're too much sometimes."

I took a sip of wine. "'Too much'?"

"Even if most actors didn't just roll their eyes at my moaning, they certainly wouldn't give me any type of praise. It's dog eat dog out there, a lot of them will do anything to make themselves look better. Even if it means fucking with your head."

"I'm just telling you the truth. And I hope I'd never do anything to fuck with anyone like that."

"I know," he said, reaching forward and giving my foot a playful slap. "Because you're one of the sweetest people I've ever met. It's beautiful."

Suddenly he grabbed my foot and pulled it onto his lap.

He ran his hand down my calf and then around my ankle. I bit my lip and inhaled quickly, trying to tamp down the rush that shot through me and landed below my waist.

"What's this?" he asked. "Is there a story behind it?"

"My tattoo?" I asked.

"Uh, yeah," he said mockingly, twisting my big toe playfully.

"Ow," I cried out, grinning. "Yes, but it's a stupid story. You don't wanna hear it, trust me."

"Yeah. I do."

He grabbed my ankle and pulled me forward a bit.

"It's embarrassing," I said. "I got it on a trip to Thailand. Could you get more cliché?"

"Does it mean anything?"

"Not in and of itself, no. But I got it with my ex. We got a matching set—his is exactly like mine. It was supposed to symbolize how we were connected—unbroken circles. I told you, it's corny."

Dennis gave me a soft smile. "I think it's kind of sweet actually."

I shrugged.

"It's only sweet if you stay unbroken. When he dumps you a year later, it's just a dumb tattoo."

I suddenly felt very self-conscious and a wave of sadness hit me. Max was the last thing I wanted to be thinking about right now. Or ever again. I lifted my foot from his lap and pulled my legs closer to me.

He nodded and his voice was softly sincere when he spoke.

"If anyone is dumb, it's him. Anyone who would break up with you, Zay, is clearly a fool. He's the one who lost out."

Not knowing what to say to that, I just blinked. I felt on the verge of tears, yet at the same time, a bursting happiness made my chest feel tight.

Dennis tossed his script to the floor and leaned over it, resting on his elbows. I saw the nape of his neck, the strong lines that disappeared below the collar of his shirt, that expanse of skin just begging to be kissed.

He looked up.

"I can't get you out of my mind," he said, his voice low and rough. The air caught in my throat. "I try to distract myself, but all I see when I close my eyes is your face. That smooth skin, those lips, in need of kissing."

He stared at me. His eyes seemed to shine in the half-darkness of my *salón*, lit only by one cheap lamp in the corner. I didn't know what to say, the wine clouded my mind, my emotions clanged around inside me, clumsy and dumb.

"What?" I managed to stammer.

Dennis smiled. "You okay, buddy? Jesus, how much of that stuff have you had?" He laughed, looking down at the script. "Your line is, 'Then why don't you kiss them?'"

"Oh, right," I said, sense returning. "My line. The script. Totally. Sorry, I spaced there for a minute."

"Maybe we should call it a night. It's been a long day."

"No, no, it's all good. I'm good. I'm fine." I objected, perhaps too hastily. I peered down at my script. "Unless you need to go, that is," I added, pointedly avoiding his gaze. "It's whatever."

He stayed silent until I was forced to lift my eyes from the script. The corner of his mouth turned up in a half-smile and he was studying me.

"No," he said finally. "I don't need to go."

I nodded.

The way he looked at me, I found myself going instantly hard. I pulled my knees up to my chest in an attempt to cover it up, but I think it just made it more obvious. He stole a glance at my crotch and then ducked his head smiling.

"You know, you don't have to worry if things... happen during rehearsals." He let his eyes wander up and down my body. "What I mean is don't be embarrassed, just go with it. I won't be offended or mind in any way. It's just natural."

I almost dropped my script.

"Yeah," I said, shrugging, trying my damnedest to sound nonchalant. "I know—I'm not—I mean, yeah, like I wouldn't be embarrassed or anything. You know—I mean— It's cool."

He nodded, biting his bottom lip, his eyes bright.

"Okay, good. Cool. Maybe we should work on the café scene then. After his parents come to visit."

"Maybe we should just get this one down," I said bashfully.

He raised a brow.

"You sure you don't want to work on something less... intense?"

"I'm fine. I mean—unless you'd rather do something else?"

He shook his head.

"I can't reach you from over there, though," he said.

"Over here?"

"Yeah. The scene calls for a make-out session. I can't kiss you if you're at the other end of the sofa. You're gonna have to come a little closer."

My erection still hadn't faded and I hesitated.

"Of course, I could always come to you," he said.

He swiftly removed the script I had placed over my crotch and tossed it aside, resting his hand on my bare knee.

"I can't get you out of my mind," he repeated the lines. "I try to distract myself, but all I see when I close my eyes is your face. That smooth skin, those lips in need of kissing."

"Then why don't you kiss them?"

And he did.

As we kissed, his hand moved from my knee and slowly up my thigh. I felt his fingers slide under the fabric of my shorts, and, surprised, I pulled away.

"No?" he asked.

Yes. Yes. Yes. I wanted to say. But what was this? Some "method acting" way of understanding his character? Was he just playing with me, experimenting?

"Do you want me to stop?"

Who cared what it was. I wanted it. Badly.

"No," I said. "Don't stop."

He smiled his crooked smile and began kissing me.

He moved with less hesitation now. His hand was inside my shorts, stroking my erect dick as his tongue played in my mouth. He palmed my balls, rolling them against each other, and then gave them a slight tug. A shiver of excitement shot through me and I moaned.

"Oh, you like that?" He murmured. His fingers danced up my cock and teased the slit, smearing the pre-cum that had begun to leak. My own hand fumbled, the angle awkward, as I searched to return the caresses. Through the thin covering of fabric my hand connected with him, hard, throbbing. I stroked as best I could and a low purr arose from the back of his throat.

"Okay," he whispered, pushing away from me as he reached down to divest himself of his pants. I pulled my shirt off, and by the time I had tossed it aside, he was crouched between my legs fully naked.

"And now," he said, sliding his hand under my backside. He lifted me and deposited me onto the sofa. He hooked his fingers in at the waist of my shorts, pulling my rear to the edge of the couch and peeling off the clothing at the same time. I fell back slightly and my legs came to rest on his shoulders so that I was completely splayed before him. He knelt on the floor and ran his hands up and down my body, his thirsty eyes drinking in every inch of flesh. I had never felt so naked, so exposed, and never had I felt so desirable.

"Oh god, Zay," he said, "I want you."

It was my turn to smile. I saw his cock jump in response.

"So have me," I said.

He practically dove, his mouth connecting with my cock and going down, down, until the full length of me was enveloped.

"Oh god," I moaned.

Experimenting? Hardly, I thought. This was not the movie star's first day on set; he had played this scene before. And played it well.

His head moved up and down, turning and angling with each stroke, burying his nose in the nest of my crotch. He kept it up until I thought I could stand it no longer and then his mouth was off. He moved, letting his tongue guide him as he nestled under my balls, licking, taking them in his mouth, one by one, and bathing them in the warmth. Then he alternated between my balls and teasing my shaft with his tongue.

I moaned, rocking my hips, pushing myself against his mouth. I wasn't usually so bold but I felt as if I were on fire, and with every thrust, he growled with satisfaction and pulled me closer. Suddenly he stopped but I couldn't open my eyes to see why. My body shuddered from the waves of sensation he had caused. Before I could wonder too long, I felt his wet fingertips at my hole. He traced and teased while his mouth went back to work, slipping just the tip of a finger in and out of my opening, pressing his thumb on that sensitive area between it and my scrotum.

I called out, arching my back, a spasm of rapture.

"No, stop, stop," I pleaded.

He did. "What's wrong? Don't you like it?"

I sat up, breathing heavily. "I like it—too much... I don't wanna. Not yet."

He licked his wet lips and chuckled.

"Let me do you," I said.

He pulled me to him for a deep kiss.

"Okay," he agreed and sat on the sofa.

As I knelt before him, it felt heady. *This is what a supplicant feels like, kneeling before the altar*, I thought.

"Look at me," Denny said in a throaty gasp. "Let me see your eyes."

I kept my mouth working and did as asked.

"Oh god," he exclaimed when our eyes met. He caressed my face. "That's beautiful."

I ran my hand over his torso, tweaking his nipple. His eyes fluttered shut, his head lolling back.

Heat rushed through me. I thrilled at the thought that I had caused such sensations in this beautiful man. That I had such power over such a magnificent creature.

I grabbed his thighs with both hands and renewed my vigor.

He threw his arms out, balling his hands into fists, arching his back then lifted his backside off the cushions and began to work his cock down my throat.

"Jesus Christ," he murmured. "You're amazing."

His praise only made me work harder. I could feel my lips stretched over my teeth, as I massaged his flesh.

"I'm so close," he gasped and I moaned in reply.

"Zay, Zay," he cried, grabbing my shoulders and pushing me off him. I looked at him, slightly confused, drunk with passion.

"Let's come together," he said.

I nodded.

He pulled me close so that our cocks crashed against one another. He wrapped his large, strong hand around them, his fingers encircling both his and my member as one. And he began to stroke, first slowly and then with passionate force. Skin against skin, man against man. I felt as if any moment we would crupt into flames. And we did, shooting hot floods onto one another's chests.

CHAPTER SIX

We didn't have any scenes together for the next couple of days. And they were long days for me. The only downside of getting the chance for such a great lead role was being in practically every scene. So no matter what the call sheet said, my name was always on it. In fact, the next time I saw Dennis was almost three days later when we had an early morning call for press. I was exhausted, still recovering from the previous evening's shoot which had gone into the wee hours and had taken a lot out of me emotionally. And I felt off, in a major way.

I wondered if the work was bleeding into my real emotional world. My character was constantly bombarded with people questioning everything about him and making him feel unsure of himself. And that same lack of surety started to reflect in me. Sure, I had been busy, I knew that. But couldn't Dennis have at least texted me or something? Our flats were just across the road from one another. Why hadn't he stopped by to check on me? When I got back from the late shoots, none of the lights were on at his place. He was likely asleep given the hour which made sense, but couldn't he have waited up for me just once? Or let me know he was thinking of me in some way?

What if he'd gotten what he wanted and now he was done? What if all he really wanted was a nice fuck and now that was taken care of, the fire had died down? But after our time alone, and that day on the bus, I couldn't shake the feeling that he was interested in more than just a fuck, too. Then again, I inwardly cringed, what if he had wanted more? That would be worse.

What if he was expecting something from me, and I fell short? What if he thought I was just some little slut trying to fuck the big movie star? Or, worse yet, what if he had been attracted to me and had been completely unimpressed? What if I was just a tourist trap on the way to the main destination?

I turned the corner and almost ran smack into him. He was standing there, on his cell phone, looking fine as hell. It seemed as if he had really dressed up for the interview. Or maybe, like me, he just wanted to feel like himself. We spent most of our time on-camera in shorts and T-shirts and terrible '80s resort wear, so to have an excuse to wear something contemporary was a godsend. And maybe, just like me, he had gotten up extra early to pick out just the right thing—something to accentuate all the best parts of his physique, snug and smooth in all the best places, just in case someone was paying attention. Someone like me.

I couldn't see his eyes, they were hidden behind the sunglasses he wore, but he smiled broadly. He lifted his hand to wave and the sunlight fanned around from behind him like a halo. *Jesus Christ*, I thought, *does heaven follow him around with his own fucking light crew?* It was unbelievable how other-worldly he could appear.

"Hey, baby, Zay's here, I gotta go," he said into the cell. "We've got this interview thing. Yeah, yeah, of course, I will. Okay. I love you too, baby."

My heart sank. He loved her too, baby. What had I been thinking? One hot night on my living room floor and he was going to be thinking of nothing but me. He had a fiancée. Someone he had been with since he was a teenager—hadn't he told me that she was his anchor, his safety, his everything? Why was I kidding myself?

"Sorry," he said. "That was Ronnie."

"Yeah," I said, trying not to sulk. "I figured."

His smile turned into a slight frown.

"Everything okay, buddy?"

Buddy. Buddy. Just your fucking buddy.

"Yeah," I muttered. "Just had a long couple of nights. I'm exhausted."

"I bet. I was wondering how you were coping with the schedule. It must have been rough—"

"Is the interview over here?" I interrupted, pointing at the cafe nearest us. "I could use something cool to drink."

"Oh, oh, okay," he said, adjusting his sunglasses. "Umm, yeah, this is it. This is the interview spot, yeah."

I nodded and turned sharply to go inside.

• • • •

"SO WE ALREADY GOT SOME time with Carlos yesterday," said the interviewer, wrapping up his spiel on the story they were here to do. "Mostly on-set, behind-the-scenes stuff and today we wanted to talk to you guys about your experience and what you've got going on in your careers. Carlos said we should talk to you together."

Dennis raised an eyebrow. "Sure, sure. Whatever you need."

"Great. I'm Jerry, by the way; nice to meet you both."

We exchanged pleasantries just as one of the cafe staff arrived with a pitcher of water.

"Perfect," said Dennis. "Just what we needed. Right, Zay? And iced too."

"Isn't it weird how they never have ice in Europe?" added Jerry.

"I guess they saw the insufferable Americans coming," said Dennis brightly with a shrug.

"Here you go," he said, grabbing my glass.

"No, it's fine, I can get it," I protested.

"I don't mind serving you," he said with a wink.

Jerry turned to the camera to film his intro bit.

"We're behind-the-scenes here in La Mancha, Spain with the stars of Carlos Pedrón's newest film, *From Cold to Hot*, James Dennis Herbert and newcomer Xavier Durand."

As Jerry did a couple of takes, Dennis replaced my now filled water glass. He leaned in close as he did, so close that his lips practically brushed against my earlobe as he whispered, "You're looking really fucking sexy today."

I inhaled sharply, the skin on my neck tingling, and a throb of desire reverberated through my body. So much for trying to play the aloof card. One compliment from him and I was shaking inside.

"So fucking sexy," Dennis added before sitting back in his chair and turning his attention to the interviewer.

I watched him expertly handle Jerry's questions, each one countered with a million-dollar smile and an easy charm. I wasn't really listening to what was being said, I just watched him. How he sat, taking up so much space, his tall frame completely hiding the chair. His legs were spread under the table and I watched as he massaged his knee, probably out of boredom, his fingertips tracing small circles around his kneecap and his thumb pressing into the rock hard flesh of his thigh, straining against the tight denim he wore. I chewed on my bottom lip.

"Zay?" I heard Dennis say and looked up.

I saw that both he and Jerry were looking at me expectantly. Oh shit. I massaged a pretend cramp in my neck, hoping I didn't appear too guilty.

"I–I'm sorry," I said. "Could you repeat the question?"

"Well," said Jerry. "They say this film is sort of a summer fling, and I was wondering if you had any similar experience—a summer fling of your own?"

I wondered if Jerry thought fucking my co-star in my rented apartment counted as a fling. I looked briefly to Dennis, who was watching me intently, but his expression was inscrutable.

I shook my head.

"No, I don't think I've had anything that would count as a summer fling before."

"Maybe not yet," said Dennis, leaning forward and blasting Jerry with his arsenal of charm. "But the summer's not over yet, right?"

He and Jerry shared a laugh, and I turned my wide-eyed flash of panic into a chuckle. I reached for my water and Dennis mimicked me, both of us taking a long sip. Just over the glass, I saw his eyes shining.

"And what about you?" Jerry asked Dennis. "Have you had a memorable summer fling?"

Dennis placed his glass on the table and traced his finger around the rim of it while he considered his answer.

"I think I'm having it right now," he said. "With this film. This whole experience. Enjoying this beautiful place, learning about this beautiful culture, all the beautiful wine and food, and, you know, getting to fall in love with this beautiful boy here." He reached over and patted my leg, letting his hand rest there. "It's not exactly the same kind of story, but I'd say this is my summer fling, yeah."

I felt frozen, my body turned to cool slick marble, the only spot of heat radiating from his hand on my thigh. I had to remind myself to breathe. Did he really just say that?

"And what about first loves?" said Jerry. "That's a big theme in this project as well according to Carlos. Xavier, do you remember your first love?"

"Yeah, Zay," said Dennis, in a gently teasing tone. "Tell us about your first love."

I licked my lips; my mouth felt dry. I scrunched up my nose and smiled.

"Ehhhh. I hate to sound like a broken record, but I'm not sure I could say. I think I need a little more time in my life to process things and really know who my first love really was."

"So it's not Max Canelo, then?" asked Jerry.

I felt as if I'd been smacked across the face.

Dennis looked slightly irritated.

"What, dude?" he said. "Why ask that?"

"It's just that Max has been making a lot of headlines as of late," said Jerry. "With his coming out. And he's mentioned that you two were an item for a couple of years. So guessing that it wasn't a true love situation, then?"

"I think he already answered that," said Dennis.

"It's just that he's been very vocal about his new relationship with Matthew Keene after being evasive about things for so long."

"Not really sure what that has to do with our film though," Dennis said pointedly.

"Oh, I don't mean to pry. I just think people will be curious about Zay's take."

Dennis leaned forward.

"No, no, look, it's okay," I said. "I'm happy for him. I am glad he is comfortable with himself. And I wish nothing but happiness for both of them."

"For both of them?" asked Jerry.

"Yes, of course. For both of them."

I gave him a very firm look and a tight smile and finally, he seemed to get the hint to move on.

The departing pleasantries were less friendly than the greeting and as the crew packed up, Dennis and I departed the café.

"What a douche," said Dennis when we were outside. "Sorry, you had to put up with that guy."

"It's fine," I said, waving away his concern.

"No, it's not. It was a real dick move to bring up your ex like that, and then keep pressing you about it."

The last thing I needed was Dennis feeling pity for me.

"Really, it's okay," I insisted. "I'm fine."

"You sure, buddy?" he asked. "You seem a little tense."

He began to massage my shoulder.

Buddy.

Is that all we were? Buddies? Friends? Old pals?

I stepped to the side, freeing my shoulder from his grasp.

"Seriously, I'm okay. I just need... I'm... Anyway, look, I've just got some stuff to do. I'll see you later on set."

"Oh, I thought maybe we could catch lunch or something before call time?"

I shrugged.

"Not right, now. Sorry. I just need to take care of something."

I turned and headed the opposite way across the square.

"Zay?" Dennis called after me.

"It's cool. It's cool," I called back over my shoulder. "Catch you later."

• • • •

"YOU HAVE MADE ME SO disappointed."

"I have?" I asked.

"Yes," replied Carlos, setting down the half-empty wine glass. He leaned back in the overstuffed chair. "You both have."

I felt stung. I glanced over at Denny who looked put out as well.

"Are we so bad?"

Carlos sat up. We were in the living room of his rented flat days later, listening to songs he had already picked or was considering for use in the soundtrack.

"I speak badly," he said, with a slight frown. "I don't mean your performance. No, *cariño*, of course. *Claro que no.* You're both superb. I couldn't ask for better if I were shooting a documentary of you falling in love."

I felt my cheeks redden. He reached for the mp3 player on the nearby side table.

"But you are lucky, no? That I changed the story to an American coming to work in his aunt's hotel in *la España*. *Porque tu español es muy—como se dice—*mediocre, *no?*"

I rolled my eyes. "*Lo siento*, Carlos."

"But never mind, *mi amor*. No, you have brought me disappointment because of a song. Watching the two of you, I remembered a song from my youth and it is perfect, I thought. That scene we shot last week of your first kiss. You remember, *claro*."

He was flipping through the music on the player.

"Do you remember the band the Wilting Wallflowers?"

We both shook our heads.

"No, *claro*. The time they last had a hit record you were both not born. *Coño*, how old I have become. *Pues*, anyway, they were a very big part of my youth. And when I saw you two together, the way you were with one another, I imagine this song in my head. And it is perfect, I think. But no, we cannot have the rights. Anyway, you should hear this song. It is called *Goner*."

He hit play and we listened. On the surface, it probably would just seem like another old '80s song. All synthesizers and programmed beats, but listening to the words, and the way the lead singer delivered the vocals it struck a chord. Carlos was right; I could see it in my mind perfectly. I could see us, together in the frame, exchanging glances, hesitant kisses, the sun spilling through the trees, the shimmer of the electronic bass, the moody voice drifting in and out, like a love-drunk phantom.

I caught Dennis staring at me. The expression on his face made it seem as if he were stranded in some limbo between dreaming and waking, and I knew, somehow, he was imagining the scene too. Our eyes locked and even though we were on opposite sides of the room, it was as if I could feel him. I tasted the salt of his skin; I could smell his musk; I could feel his hands on my cock, his mouth on mine. The edges of my vision started to fade away until all I saw was his face. It was as if the image of him was burnt into me; I could close my eyes and see him perfectly etched on the back of my eyelids.

The music stopped. We both turned to Carlos, who was watching us closely.

"Can I get a copy of that?" asked Dennis.

Carlos smiled slightly. "I already gifted you both the album. On the mp3. Check your emails." He lifted the wine glass and took a sip. "Later," he added. "When you are not so distracted, eh?"

• • • •

DENNIS LEFT THE ROOM, but I lingered behind. I watched Carlos as he organized some papers on his desk. After a few moments, he gave me his attention. Smiling softly, he tilted his head and raised his eyebrows.

He knew I wanted to ask him something; he had a way of knowing exactly what the situation was, even if he did not always let on. And I did want to talk to him, but even I wasn't sure what I wanted to talk about. He waited.

"What was it like?" I asked. "Coming back to La Mancha. Since the story ended—I mean, the real summer that you based the film on."

He folded his hands in front of him.

"But I have been back many times since then."

"But I mean, with this film. You said you made it look exactly like it did when you were a teenager. That must have been strange, like stepping back in time."

He nodded. "In a way. But this time I was in control, moving around all the little pieces, making things happen as I wanted them to. *Un mundo de fantasías*. And really, it has never changed much here."

"You said you wanted to give it a happy ending this time. So it was not happy before?"

"No, no, of course not. It was hard, very hard."

I nodded. "I want to make sure that comes through—not to take the happy-ending for granted. The '80s were not that long ago. I want them to know it was not an easy thing to have."

He looked at me for a moment.

"But, *mi amor*, love is never easy, no matter who you are. Most of the time at the very least it takes *transigencia,* the compromise, *sí*? And other times it requires you to give up everything for it. Complete sacrifice.

"Things have changed, yes. New York City, Los Angeles, even this little village where I grew up have become bigger, more open. But even when the world changes, people can be the same inside. *Me entiendes*? What I mean to say is that it is a scary thing to be yourself in a way that does not fit to the normal, to what people expect of you. Even if those people are people you—*pues*, especially if they are the people you love. I am a famous movie director now, yes. I am celebrated in my country and over the world. But still, when I walk down these streets, I see some of the same looks I saw thirty, forty years ago. Maybe they hide behind smiles now, maybe they call out to me to say hello. But really, have they changed? *Claro que no.*

"But I do not love this village because it has changed. I love it because it is a part of me. It doesn't have to love me back for me to love it. And the people here do not have to love me back for me to love them. Their—how do you say?—their limitations are their own problem that they must solve. The difference is that now, now I know this. Now I know that is love, *mi amor interior*, that keeps me from getting hurt. My love is *my* love to give freely. Do I want it returned? *Por supuesto!* But even if it is not it still means something to me. The act of loving still makes me a better person. I just have to remember not to let the coldness I receive in reply make me doubt myself. That has nothing to do with my love. Do you understand what I mean?"

I nodded slowly, not entirely sure that I did understand but feeling like something was becoming clearer.

"Maybe one day they will see me for what I truly am," he continued. "Not a filmmaker, not a celebrity, not a *maricón*, not even that strange little boy who followed his aunt around like a lost little bird. Maybe one day they will simply see me and it will be enough. Maybe not. But this is the best I can hope for. To be able to be honest. For me to say here is this gift of my love. Maybe you do not appreciate it now, maybe you never will. Maybe you will look back when we are both old and falling apart and realize what you have missed. But, *a pesar de todo*, it is the truth. And being truthful about love can never be wrong."

He was right, that did sound frightening. I'd given my love freely before, without any expectations, and it had come back to hurt me terribly. I knew he was probably right, but I wasn't sure I could take that risk again. What doesn't kill you only makes you stronger, the cliché says. But what if it kills you? What if it crushes your heart beyond repair? Was it worth finding out?

"I hope that helps you a little bit," said Carlos. "To understand your character, I mean."

I looked at him. His smile was innocuous, placid even, but his eyes seemed to gleam. I felt as if he was reading my thoughts.

"Yes." I nodded. "It has helped very much."

As I left the room, I chewed on my bottom lip and prayed that it actually had.

CHAPTER SEVEN

They called it Glamor Central. Since they were shooting on location for a long schedule, the production had rented a lot of local spaces so that they didn't have to have trailers and intrude on the landscape. It was a pleasant change, not being cooped up within those fiberglass walls.

One of the largest spaces they rented was a former dance studio that had recently closed, having moved to a bigger building, and the film made it the main hall for hair, makeup, and wardrobe. It was a perfect fit. Big, bright, airy, with tons of mirrors all around. And since it was one of the few buildings they'd rented with dependable A/C, it had kind of become the main hangout for the cast and crew as well. It was a blisteringly hot summer and even those who liked the heat needed some respite every now and then. The crew had even pulled in a couple of couches and cordoned off a piece of the main studio as a lounge spot.

Dennis and I were seated near each other, both getting our hair done for the upcoming afternoon shoot. Most of the crew were on break, *siesta* time, to escape the worst heat of the day after a morning shoot with some of the other players. Carlos and the DP and a few of the tech crew were out shooting some B-roll.

Dennis stopped scrolling on his tablet and looked up.

"So this Max Lanelo guy is really getting a lot of press," he said.

"Max?" I was caught off guard. Why did his name keep coming up? "What do you mean?"

"Sorry, we don't have to talk about him. It's just there's this article that just popped up in my news alerts where he mentions you."

"He mentioned me?"

"Yeah, he's talking about this tattoo he got to commemorate his new phase in life. And he says that you inspired him to come out."

I rolled my eyes. "'Inspired him'? Oh, gimme a fucking break."

"What do you mean? That's not a good thing?"

"*Coño*!" A deep voice boomed as the front door opened. In came Liberto, the first assistant camera. His face was screwed up in a frown and he seemed aggravated.

I liked Liberto. We hadn't had much time together off set, but he seemed really cool. And, to be completely honest, he was fine as hell. He was from New York too, like me; I wasn't sure where exactly, but he had the accent and I liked hearing it. And I always caught him giving me certain looks between takes.

"I'm sweating like a fiend," he announced. "It's like walking through flames out there. I'm drenched." He smiled at the wardrobe lady. "Lisette, you got a T-shirt I can change into? Just for the rest of the day."

Liberto peeled off the damp shirt he was wearing. I couldn't help but notice his sculpted body. His abs were chiseled and he had that serious "V." And he was glistening. I tried not to stare but, fuck, it made me realize how worked up I'd been. I was always piqued but didn't have any release. Dennis and I hadn't hung out for any length of time since we'd first hooked up. I was beginning to realize he must have changed his mind about me.

Liberto casually turned his head and made eye contact with me in the mirror. He raised his chin in a nod of acknowledgment and one side of his mouth lifted in a half-smile.

"Wassup, *papo*?" he said.

"Hey, Liberto."

"Ready for this afternoon's shoot?" he asked.

"Hope so," I said, shrugging. "If I can stay cool."

"Yeah," he agreed. He took the crumpled T-shirt he had just removed and rubbed it all over his torso. He glanced back up at me. "It's definitely hot."

We locked eyes in the mirror and he smiled. I smiled back and nodded, trying not to blush as I averted my eyes.

"Gimme a fucking break," said Dennis.

I was startled. Dennis was watching Liberto in the mirror as if he were tracking him. His entire posture suggested he was ready to pounce. Liberto gave him an inscrutable smirk and turned toward the wardrobe crew.

"Sorry?" I asked.

Dennis blinked at me as if trying to remember what he had said. I bit back a smile. If I hadn't known any better, I could have sworn he was jealous.

"Oh, you said gimme a break. About this Max dude. You didn't seem to be too happy about him saying you inspired him."

"Oh, him. Yeah, not so much."

Dennis set his tablet down.

"But isn't that sort of a compliment, though? I mean, he was struggling with something and you inspired him to deal with it."

I studied my fingernails, trying to think of the best way to say what I was feeling without sounding like the bitter ex.

"See, I was already out when I started dating him. But I had to pretend to be single the whole time because he wasn't ready. And, at first, I thought I was cool with that. But in a lot of ways, it felt like I was going back in the closet. I couldn't talk about the guy I was dating—the guy I thought I was in love with. I was always watching what I said or talking around the subject or, you know, even pretending like we weren't on trips together—that it was just for work or whatever."

He leaned forward in his chair.

"Maybe it's not about being closeted. Maybe it's about still figuring out who you are. It's not easy for some people in the most normal of circumstances, but especially not with all the attention and pressure to be a certain thing we get—in the industry, I mean."

"Of course, I get that. I dealt with some of the same stuff myself. And he wasn't the first guy I dated that was in the closet. Which was part of the reason I was willing to give that kind of space. But, I dunno, it's like a slap in the face."

I pressed the palms of my hands to my eyes and made a sort of growling noise in jest. I didn't want Dennis to see me get emotional about this subject, but it was still hard to articulate.

"Ehh. It just feels like I was inadequate, I guess. I was the one there in the trenches with him. Comforting him in the middle of the night when he cried about the pressure; soothing him, whispering to him in private when he was having anxiety attacks at public events. Pretending to his parents that I was just his friend or roommate when it was plainly obvious they didn't buy it for a moment. The awkwardness, the discomfort. I was there for all that. And I guess it made him stronger? Which I appreciate in hindsight. But when he was strong enough, he chose someone else. And I'm just, like, why wasn't I enough? It fucks with you." I chewed on my bottom lip. "I mean, yeah. Whatever," I added with a shrug.

"I think you're looking at it all wrong," said Dennis quietly.

He was staring at me in the mirror. "Maybe," he continued, "his feelings for you were so deep that they scared the shit out of him. Maybe he was afraid that if he opened up to you completely, he'd be a goner. Maybe that was just so frightening that he ran away from it. And then found something that was less dangerous to lose—something that wouldn't cost him too much if it ended—something that was easier to lose."

I didn't know what to say to that. There was something in his eyes that reminded me of that bus ride. Something about his inflection. As if he wanted me to ask him a question, but I didn't know what the question was.

"Yeah. Maybe," I said.

"Or maybe you just need to pick better guys, *papi*." Liberto was suddenly between us. He posed in front of the mirror, straightening his new T-shirt, a little tighter than necessity probably demanded. He smoothed out his eyebrows. "You should stop letting these little boys into your life and get yourself a *real* man. That's what I think. A real man knows what he wants and isn't afraid of saying so."

With one last ruffle of his hair, Liberto wet his lips and winked at me. I couldn't help but let out a small chuckle. Liberto certainly didn't feel the need to mince words.

"See you on set, pa," he said, giving me a light, playful punch to the shoulder.

"Who the fuck is that guy anyway?" snapped Dennis as soon as the door closed.

"You don't remember Liberto?" asked Tricia, Dennis's hair person, as she approached to make final checks. "We worked with him a couple of years ago on that action film. He was the second AC. I think you worked with him a couple of times actually."

Dennis cut his eye at me.

"Oh yeah," he said nonchalantly. "Guess he's just easy to forget."

• • • •

"SO WHEN DO I GET TO meet that-hot-guy-from?"

Jaelyn had wrapped her TV show and had written to let me know she was headed to Europe to film a small part in a buddy comedy. Luckily the overlap coincided with a four-day break we had in shooting so she was able to re-route her travels to Spain to come visit.

"That-hot-guy-from?" I asked.

"Don't play dumb."

"I assume you're talking about Denny?"

"Oh, 'Denny,' huh? And of course, I am. But everybody calls him '*that-hot-guy-from*' dot dot dot. When I told everyone what you were working on they were like, Oh! You mean that-hot-guy-from *Call Waiting*—or that-hot-guy-from *Tidal Wave*."

The waiter brought our cocktails and we thanked him happily.

"Dennis is actually an excellent actor, you know."

"Sure," she agreed, sipping on her *tinto de verano*. "But, come on, look at him. Does it really matter if he can act?"

"Isn't that kind of sexist?"

"Really, bitch?"

She gave me a look and I laughed.

"Well, that's exactly why he's doing this film—to prove to everyone that he is a legit actor and not just a pretty face."

"And an amazing ass. Don't forget that."

"Jaelyn!"

"I'm just saying! Zaddy is thicc. Okay, okay, I'll chill. I didn't know you were such a fangirl. I'm just joking."

"Anyway, he's out of town for a bit. He got a role lined up so his agent had him fly to London for a few days to meet with people. You'll see him tomorrow at dinner."

"So I don't get to watch the two of you do a scene together? That sucks."

"Well, you could always stay longer."

"I wish! I've only got these few days before I have to be in Paris."

"Ah, *pobresito*," I teased her. "'I just *have* to be in Paris.' Miss World Traveler over here."

"Well, you know," she said with an exaggerated flip of her hair. "One does what one can."

• • • •

THE NEXT NIGHT ALL the cast and crew were gathered at *El Ingenioso Hidalgo*, a favorite local restaurant of Carlos's. It had been a nice short break in our schedule but we were all ready to get back to work. This marked the halfway point of the shoot, and we were ahead of schedule and on budget. Carlos was full of gratitude and love, so the drinks flowed freely and the food kept coming. Some of the locals seemed aggravated by our presence on a daily basis, but not the business people. They loved the movie star dollars we spent.

Everyone adored Jaelyn, as usual, and in a matter of a couple of days, she had become part of the family. She was practicing her French on the actress who played my aunt when I saw the door open and Dennis breeze in, running late.

It had only been a few days but seeing him made my heart jump. I bounced out of my seat to greet him, painfully aware of what my enthusiasm must have looked like. But before I had a chance to worry much about it he was wrapping his arms around me in a bear hug.

"God, I missed you, man," he said quietly. He held me by the shoulders and peered into my face, smiling. He glanced around and announced in a louder voice, "Hey, everybody, I missed you guys!"

We sat.

"I thought that taxi would never get here. Am I very late?" he asked.

"No, they just brought out the *third round* of small plates," I said.

"And the *cuchifritos*," added Jaelyn. "My old roommate from the city was Puerto Rican and his *abuela* used to make that for us, but it never tasted this good. Clearly some Manchego magic at work."

Dennis laughed. "You must be Jaelyn."

"The one and only," she answered, extending her hand.

"Thank goodness," I added.

Jaelyn cut her eye at me and lifted her hand in a mock slap, prompting more laughter from Dennis.

"It's so good to be back," he said.

"You've only been gone two days, *mi amor*," said Carlos. "Hardly time to miss us, I think."

"I know, but it was strange leaving here. I was surprised. This feels like home already. I love London but I got there and I was like, where is the sunshine, where are my peoples?"

He winked at me.

"So listen, Jaelyn," said Dennis. "I know you two go way back so I'm going to need all the dirt on our buddy, Zay, here. All the gory details."

"Oh, I'm happy to oblige," she answered. "But it's pretty boring stuff, I'm sad to say. Xavier is just so nice. It's kind of sickening, really."

"I bet he has a freaky side," said Dennis. "Maybe he'll surprise you one day."

Jaelyn gave me a sly look.

"Yeah," she said. "Maybe he'll surprise us both."

"Why you go audition for this crap anyway?" interrupted Carlos from across the table. "You told me you wanted to be an artist. And now more of this studio shit? *Esa mierda!*"

"I do want to be an artist," Dennis replied with an exasperated sigh. "But this *studio shit* pays a lot of money, Carlos."

"Why you need so much money? For cars? Women? *Por favor*, I hope not for *las drogas*. You are not a *yunkie, mi amor? Ojalá que no.* It is terrible for the complexion."

Denny laughed and gave him the middle finger.

"I'll have you know it's for my mom, actually. She's been really sick and I need the money to help pay for her treatments. I want to give her the best."

"Of course, *cariño*. I am sorry for joking."

"No, it's okay."

"Is she okay now?" I asked.

"She's in recovery and doing her best, but it takes its toll. She's a strong lady—she's got a lot of fight in her. She's been a CNA for years, working the night shift. The pay isn't great and the benefits are even worse. It's ironic that she spends all her working hours taking care of other people and making sure they get the proper medical attention, but she can't even afford it for herself. But she's proud—she didn't even tell me until it was pretty bad."

"I will pray for her," said Carlos.

"She would like that. She very much believes in prayer." He turned to Jaelyn and me. "Little old Southern lady, really old school. Her two favorite things are Jesus and hush puppies."

Jaelyn grimaced. "So she's going to love this movie then, huh."

"Oh, she'll never see this movie."

"I would like to meet your mother," said Carlos. "I will convince her to see the movie. I think she will love me."

"You know what; I think she actually would love you. That's the sad part."

"*Pues, claro, mi amor*. I am extremely loveable."

. . . .

OVERLY SATED AND DRUNK, we left the restaurant a couple of hours later.

"We're still gonna check out that club, right?" asked Jaelyn.

"Sure thing," I said. "I could use some dancing to burn through all these delicious calories."

"Cool, we'd better go or we'll miss the train."

"Wait, wait, what's going on?" asked Dennis.

"Oh, one of the crew was telling us about this club in the city," explained Jaelyn. "It's apparently the only decent place to go if you really wanna dance. It's like practically an hour away, so we're gonna catch the train there."

"Oh, I'm so down," declared Denny.

"Awesome!" cried Jaelyn.

"You sure?" I interjected. "You know, it's... well, it's a gay club."

"So what?" asked Dennis, biting his bottom lip. "Let's go dancing, dude."

I smiled.

"Cool, let's do it."

CHAPTER EIGHT

Gospel-tinged wails and bass-thumping so loudly I could barely hear myself think wrapped themselves around me. Bodies were crammed against one another in this small, ancient club. But it didn't matter. People were letting themselves go; letting themselves get lost; letting the mood take over. It wasn't a New York or LA club, with lighting rigs and video screens screaming from every angle, but it was filled to the brim with people who wanted to be here, who needed to be here, who sought this place out for maybe the only chance they could find to be themselves. A few go-go boys danced on tiny, shoddily constructed platforms, one atop the end of the bar itself. A drag queen in a cheap multicolored wig and too-tight dress bounced beside the DJ shouting things into a microphone that I could barely hear and certainly not understand. But it didn't matter.

The only thing I saw was Dennis anyway. He beamed from the moment we walked in, and his happiness was infectious. The three of us found a spot and danced in a tight little clique, but he stayed as close to me as he possibly could. He wasn't the greatest dancer, but he didn't let it stop him. He rolled his hips, threw his hands around wildly, and shook his head to the beat. He pressed up against me and it made me laugh. But despite his awkward steps and questionable rhythm, I had never wanted him more. He looked so free, so blissed-out. It felt as if we had been thrown into some other dimension that we might not make it back from, and I was happy to be lost.

"Okay, I'm about to faint," Jae leaned close to my ear and yelled over the music. "I need a drink. Water. The tears of an angel. Some kinda hydration needs to be happening."

"I'll get us some drinks," I said.

She kissed me on the cheek and fell back into dancing. I tried to find a path through the mash of bodies.

"Hey, hey, hey," Dennis said, grabbing me by the waist. "Where are you going?"

"Just to get drinks. What do you want?"

"I don't care," he said, looking at me with what I swore was pure adoration. "Just hurry back."

I leaned in to kiss him, and then caught myself. We were in public, not inside our flats, and not in character, safely hidden in fiction.

Dennis leaned toward me too, but there was hesitation. If there was a move to be made, I would have to make it. But what if I was wrong? What if he couldn't handle something like that in public, in front of people? What if he pushed me away? That would crush me and I couldn't take that chance.

If only you would just kiss me; just let me know it was okay, I thought.

I patted him on the chest.

"I'll be right back, promise."

. . . .

I CAUGHT SIGHT OF MYSELF in the mirrored back of the bar. The uncertainty and anxiety didn't read on me, which was good to know. In fact, I was damn near glowing. I laughed at myself. Like it or not, confused or not, I clearly was happy to be here. Just being around that man made me light up.

"Xavier?"

I turned, surprised to hear my name. It was Liberto.

"Ayyy, *papi*," he exclaimed pulling me into a tight hug. "I didn't know you knew about this place. You should have told me. I would have been glad to give you a ride."

The bartender deposited my three drink orders on the bar.

"Oh, we took the train."

"'We'?"

"Yeah, me and my friends Jaelyn and Dennis."

"Dennis is here too? That's a surprise."

I shrugged. "He likes to dance."

Liberto gave me a sly look.

"Hmmm. Yes." He reached for one of the drinks. "Let me give you a hand with those."

"Thanks," I said.

Liberto quickly insinuated himself in our group, mostly dancing with Jaelyn. She was glad to have a partner and put all her dance skills to use. She threw it back on Liberto, wrapped a leg around his thigh, pulled and tugged him in every way imaginable. Dennis loved it and cheered her on, hooting and clapping. Pretty soon her dancing began to suspiciously resemble a number from her musical television show.

"Okay, Beyoncé," I leaned in to yell at her. "We get it, you've got moves!"

"Don't judge me," she cried, laughing.

The beat changed up and a new song started.

We grabbed one another's hands, mouths open, eyes wide and jumped in unison.

"That's our song!" Jaelyn whooped and pulled me to her.

We grooved to the music. We were feeling ourselves, and as she gave it to me, I gave it back just as good. I saw Dennis watching us and I winked at him. We jammed together until the beat started to slow and a more seductive tune came into the mix.

"Okay, pretty boy," Jaelyn said. "Hydration."

And she left me to go fetch more drinks. The rhythm was slinky and I was in the spot, feeling a groove, so I just stayed there dancing by myself. Dennis, who had been bopping along near us, slowed to a stop as he watched me dance. I loved the feeling of his eyes on me, loved the idea that watching me might be exciting him, and it spurred me on. I let my hands run over my body as I danced and closed my eyes.

I imagined Dennis with his arms around me, and that my hands were his. I threw my head back and rolled my hips; thinking of how I would tease him. A hand slid around my waist and someone pressed against my backside. I moved back into it, grinding my hips.

"*Sí, baby, eso*," I heard Liberto purr.

Dennis watched us, and though the first jab of instinct told me to break away from Liberto, something kept me there instead. A mix of emotions seemed to wash over Dennis - troubled, lustful, and even a little angry. It turned me on that he seemed so enraptured by me, and at the same time, it annoyed me that he didn't move in, be the one to wrap his arm around me. Claim me as his. I was dancing for him, after all; he had to know that. Liberto's body was responding to me. His hands roamed, grabbing my hips then running under my shirt and caressing my stomach. I felt his lips brushing the back of my neck. Dennis noticed too and raised his chin, his expression tight. His breath seemed to deepen as he watched Liberto kiss my neck, almost as if he were trying to control himself. But I wanted him to lose that control, to give in to whatever that roiling passion was that he could hardly contain. Letting my head fall back against Liberto's shoulder, I met Denny's gaze. I let my eyes travel slowly up and down his body, taunting him, presenting myself, the demand pulsing through my veins, hoping he would respond.

"Damn, it's packed in here," cried Jaelyn as she was suddenly between us, two drinks in each hand. "Quick, take them before I almost drop them again."

Dennis grabbed his glass and knocked it back in one gulp. "Thanks," he said.

"And I thought I was thirsty," said Jaelyn.

"Hey, Zay," Dennis said, grabbing me by the arm roughly and pulling me toward him. "Bathroom break?"

He led me into the back of the club, down a hallway to where the lavatory was. It was a one-person affair and the door was locked, occupied. We fell against the wall to wait. He didn't look at me as we waited and I wasn't sure what to say, so I said nothing. I was a little shocked by the force with which he had wrenched me from the dance floor.

"So, you and Liberto," he finally said. "Didn't know you guys were so close."

"We're not," I answered. "I don't know him any more than you do."

He squinted. "Umm, I think you're a little more intimately familiar with him than me."

"We were just dancing," I said.

But when I heard the tone of my voice, I felt annoyed with myself. Why did I feel guilty? I could dance with whomever I wanted. And certainly, Dennis, of all people, didn't have the right to be jealous, did he? Not considering what this was.

"Yeah, I noticed," he said. "He's a good dancer. Much better than me."

I shrugged and didn't respond.

The door to the bathroom opened. Dennis headed in, pausing just inside the threshold.

"There's enough room in here for two if you don't want to wait."

A small storm swelled within me. I was partly annoyed at him, partly thrilled that he was trying to coerce me like this, and partly angry at myself for even caring about any of the above.

I shook my head.

"I'm okay. I'll wait."

When I stepped back into the hallway after using the restroom myself shortly after, Dennis was waiting.

"So you wanna stick around?" he asked me.

"Yeah. I'm having a good time."

He turned away, nodding, his tongue in his cheek and his jaw set.

"Are you upset?" I asked.

He shook his head.

"You sure? Because you looked kinda pissed off."

He fell onto the wall beside me, our shoulders touching.

"I'm not pissed off," he said. He brushed his fingers against mine. "I'm just... I don't know what I am. Or why." He sighed heavily. "This place is cool—I mean, okay, this place is *not* cool.

But I thought it would be cool to come here with you. Just us. And, you know, just get to be."

"Get to be what?" I asked.

"Just be." He turned, resting one arm on the wall above my head, and leaned close. "I couldn't resist the idea of dancing with you all night. Who could?"

He lifted my chin and moved in to kiss me. But just then, before our lips connected, his phone rang. It was a ringtone I'd heard many times. He swore and grabbed for it in his pocket. Instantly, I felt deflated. And, as much as I was ashamed to admit it, hurt.

"Fuck," he said. "I totally forgot to call. One sec," he said to me, holding up his hand. "Hey Ronnie," he said, answering the call. "I know, I'm sorry, baby. I just rushed back and we were busy. Huh? Oh, the music. We're in the middle of shooting right now—it's like a party scene, you know. What's that? I've missed you too, baby. Sure, sure, of course, I can talk—just let me go somewhere quieter."

I turned and headed back to the dance floor.

"Hey, Zay," he said, covering the phone. "Sorry."

I threw up my hand without turning around.

"No problem."

I stalked back to the dance floor. What kind of fool was I? Here I was, actually getting off on the fact that he had the nerve to act jealous. For what reason? Did I actually think I was special to him? I was the bit on the side. And I had the nerve to know it, to go along with it. What a fool I had allowed myself to become. The romance was the movie we were shooting, and I was letting it bleed into reality. As soon as the director yelled cut it would all be over, and I would be left looking like a chump.

Jaelyn sidled up to me, swaying her hips to the music.

"Where's your boyfriend?" she asked.

"He's not my fucking boyfriend," I said through gritted teeth.

"Okay, sorry. You were just gone so long I wasn't sure if I'd see either of you for a while," she said with a wink, trying to ease the atmosphere.

I opened my mouth to reply but was interrupted by Liberto insinuating himself between us.

"He's back," said Liberto. "And alone this time."

"Most definitely alone," I said with a nod.

Liberto smiled mischievously and pulled me to him. A couple of ladies came up and claimed Jaelyn as their dance partner and she happily joined them. The music throbbed on, the bass reverberating against the ancient plaster walls. *Fuck it*, I thought. I'd come here to dance and I was going to dance. I liked the feel of Liberto's body on mine. If Dennis couldn't be man enough to let me know what he really wanted from me, Liberto seemed to have no qualms. Why was I twisting myself into knots for a guy who brushed me aside for a phone call? I grabbed the drink Liberto was holding and gulped it down. He smiled and pressed his mouth by my ear.

"Can I get you another?"

I shook my head and instead pressed my lips on his. His surprise quickly passed and he kissed me back hard. He didn't hesitate to let his tongue go where it wanted. He slid his hands down and grabbed my ass, hard, and I liked it. I pushed myself against the growing bulge in his jeans.

I felt an urgent tapping on my shoulder. I ignored it but it just got more aggressive until I was forced to break away from Liberto, blinking. Dennis was standing beside us. He jerked his chin, indicating I should come off the dance floor. I turned back to Liberto.

"Looks like the movie star is back," he said with a smirk.

"Movie star? I think you mean Drama Queen." I rolled my eyes.

Dennis tugged on my shoulder.

"What?" I exclaimed fiercely.

"Can I talk to you?" he asked.

"Now?"

"Yes. Now. Please."

I felt Liberto's fingers graze my neck. "It's okay, *pa*, go ahead. I'll wait."

I gave Liberto a deep, long kiss. I hoped Dennis had a good vantage point.

"Be right back," I told Liberto, and he winked at me.

Back at the bar, Dennis pulled me onto a stool and sat beside me.

"I just wanted to apologize for the phone call—" he began.

"Why should you apologize?" I asked curtly.

"I didn't want it to interrupt. But I had promised her I would call from London, and—"

"Please," I interrupted. "Do anything but offer me an explanation. I don't think I can bear it."

"Is that why you're out there doing that?" Now his voice was taut.

"Doing what exactly?"

"Hanging all over Liberto like that."

"I was dancing."

"Oh, come on. That dude is just trying to fuck you."

"Okay," I guffawed. "And is that so bad? At least he knows what he wants from me."

"What is that supposed to mean?"

I got up. "I came here to have a good time."

"So did I," he said, grabbing my arm. "With you."

"So come dance with us then," I said. "I'm sure Liberto wouldn't mind."

He flinched and I felt a tug in my chest. I was being too bitchy. But damn it, I had every reason. He was the one playing games.

He shook his head.

"It's early enough," he said. "I think I can still catch the train back to the village."

I wanted to grab him by the shirt and yell at him. *No, you stupid asshole, say I'm not allowed to dance with Liberto. Say I'm yours and no one else's. Make me come with you; don't let me walk away!*

But I just shrugged.

"See you at work, Dennis," I said and quickly turned back to the dance floor before I could see his reaction.

CHAPTER NINE

A couple of hours later, Jaelyn and I piled into Liberto's rental car. The night air felt good and I stuck my arm out of the window as we rode, moving it like a wave. It was dark outside, so dark, in that way only the countryside can be dark. Darkness all around with only the stars for any light. The lights of the train tracks were even shut off at this point. I thought of Dennis, alone in the train, riding back to the village, looking out on these same pitch-black fields.

Was he thinking of me now? Or was he on the phone, talking to her, telling her all about his days in Spain? Was he pissed at me? Pissed that his piece on the side had screwed up his sure thing of getting laid tonight? Was he actually jealous, envious that I had chosen Liberto over him? Or was he asleep in his bed, oblivious to the fact that even now, hours later, in the unconquerable darkness of midnight, I was completely wrapped up in thoughts of him?

"You're at the hotel, right?" Liberto asked Jaelyn. "I can drop you there."

"That's perfect," she said from the back seat.

"Actually, you can just drop us both in the *Cuadrado de María*. I'll walk Jae to her hotel. I could use some air."

I saw Jaelyn screw up her face in the rearview mirror.

"It's cool, Zay," Liberto said. "I can take you back to your place." He licked his lips, adding, "Or wherever."

"Sorry," I said, forcing a yawn. "I'm just really exhausted and we have the early shoot tomorrow and I drank too much, you know."

He gave me a look and sighed.

Liberto stopped the car by the square and reached over, taking my phone from my hand. He typed something and handed it back to me.

"There," he said. "Now you have my number. So if you want to chill sometime, just hit me up."

I smiled and nodded. "Definitely."

He leaned over and kissed me gently on the cheek.

"*Buenas noches, papi.*"

As we watched his car pull away, Jaelyn punched my arm.

"What the hell was that?" she snapped.

"What?"

"*Whaaat?*" she mocked. "Sexy Deep Voice that just drove off, you know what. He was so into you, and you completely dissed him."

We began the walk to her hotel.

"I know. I just— I'm tired. And I know I'm gonna be so hungover tomorrow."

"Hungover, my ass. Hung up, more like."

"Hung up?"

"Yep. Hung up."

"What are you talking about?"

"I'm   talking   about that-hot-guy-from-couldn't-stop-looking-at-you-all-night-long? Don't play dumb, sis."

"Oh, whatever," I grumbled. "He is otherwise occupied."

"What's that mean?"

"He's straight. Or something. And it's stupid."

"He told you that?"

"He told me he has a fiancée."

"Okay, so it's complicated. But that doesn't mean he's not into you. It couldn't be more obvious."

"His fiancée is a woman, Jae. So..."

"Don't be that limited asshole, Zay. Bisexuals do exist. Don't negate their experiences just because they don't fit into your narrow binary."

I gave her a look and she returned it, lips pursed.

"Okay, fine, you're right," I said. "Don't get all Tumblr Generation on me. Of course, bi people exist. It's just... I mean, he— I don't know!"

I raked my hands through my hair, growling in frustration.

"Do you really think he's into me?" I asked.

Jaelyn laughed.

"Are you serious right now? Dude came back from London, and when he walked in the door he saw no one else in that restaurant. Not even me. Not a glance. And you know I looked good as hell tonight."

I laughed.

"Plus, he was all over you at the club. And then you guys had your little lesbian couple at prom moment at the bar all because Berto Sexy Voice was pushing up on you. Who, by the way, really could have dropped us at my hotel. I *am* in heels, bitch."

She stopped and removed said heels, handing them to me, and we continued to walk.

"Have you guys hooked up?" she asked.

"No," I answered quickly.

"So you're just gonna completely lie to me then?"

"I'm not lying." She gave me a look. "Okay, fine. But it's not like we—I mean, we only—"

"Save it for your diary, girl."

"You know I sometimes hate you, right?" I said teasingly.

"Naturally. But, for real, isn't it kind of a weird move for a closet case to take a movie where he's playing gay? I mean, you'd think he'd be worried people would make assumptions. Unless it's like a double bluff. Because even when you're completely hetero, a lot of dunderheads think, oh, they must be gay. They even assume I'm actually in love with that asshole who plays my boyfriend on the show. As if."

"I don't think closet case is fair. Not exactly. It's complicated, I think."

"Oh, so now you're defending your boyfriend?"

"Number one, I hate you. Number two, weren't you just making the case against bisexual erasure?"

"Touché."

"But, seriously. I think, with him, maybe it's just— I don't know. It's just that sometimes you unconsciously go looking for things that make you scared. Sometimes it's the closest thing to feeling alive. Even if you know it can't end like you want it to, it's worth it just to have that feeling for a short time. To fool yourself into thinking it's real. You know?"

Jaelyn gave me a look.

"You know it doesn't make it worse that you're a guy," she said.

"What?"

"I mean if you were one of my girlfriends I'd still be encouraging you."

I clucked my tongue.

"Encouraging them to be a homewrecker?"

"Oh please," she said. "There's hardly a home to wreck. They've had, like, the longest engagement in recorded history. No one actually believes they're getting married at this point."

"How do you know that?"

"Look, I'm not saying the whole thing is PR or anything, but they got engaged when they were both having tremendous career breakthroughs. Hell, she got half a million new followers during her 'wedding plans' phase. Her brand skyrocketed and so did his. I'm not saying they did it for the likes, but maybe they were just riding the wave of happiness and went for it. To sort of seal the deal, make the picture-perfect coupledom actually perfect. But that was five years ago. That's an eternity in the world of pop culture. No one even remembers."

"I remember," I said defensively.

But in truth my mind wandered back to those words Dennis had said, sentiments too similar, almost exactly, to what Jae was describing. It was scary how close to home it hit.

"And I'm not telling you to wreck a relationship," Jae continued. "I'm telling you, you need to pursue the possibility. Connections don't come along that often, not real, deep ones at least. And definitely not mutual ones. If they break up because his heart is now with you, it doesn't make it more scandalous or dirty because it happened with a guy instead of another girl."

"I'm not so sure social media would agree with you. Or the industry."

"Maybe not. But fuck them. I'm not talking about them. I'm talking about *you*. You're not manipulating some poor stupid straight boy. That's a full-grown man who knows what he likes, even if he's too timid to admit it."

I smirked.

"Not so sure timidity is his problem."

"More to my point, then," Jaelyn said with a smile.

We stopped walking. She put her hand on my cheek.

"Just be happy, Zay. That's all I'm saying. I haven't seen you this wrapped up in someone since Max. And I know that's scary. But don't let being afraid make you lonely; you deserve better than that. You know that, right?"

I nodded.

"Good. Now give me back my heels. We're finally at my damn hotel."

· · · ·

I TOOK THE LONG WAY back from Jaelyn's hotel, trying to absorb the calm of the night and clear my head from the mire of emotions I had trampled through earlier. People milled around the village, glad for the cooler temperatures post-sunset. There were tourists in their diaphanous linen shirts and trousers, as well as locals, smiling and chatting away as they waved to the neighbors they knew and the intruders, like me, who they didn't. Two old ladies, both round-faced and adorable, passed me in their traditional skirts—the colorful lines of woven wool that made up their *refajos* bright even in the darkness. From somewhere a few avenues over, the skipping guitar strains of a *fandango* floated through the air as the singer undulated her voice to match.

The air turned sharply colder and as I moved onto the avenue where Dennis and I were staying, I shivered. As I neared my place, I couldn't help but glance across the street. I was surprised to see Dennis on the small patio out front, smoking.

I paused. He lifted his chin and waved me over. *I should just wave goodnight and go to bed*, I told myself, even as my feet took me quickly across the narrow street.

"You're still up?" I said as I approached him.

He nodded and handed me the joint he was smoking. I took a drag.

"Yep," he said.

"Kinda cold out, isn't it?"

He shrugged. "I was waiting."

"For what?"

"You."

He reached for my hand, entwining our fingers. I didn't resist.

"I'm sorry about earlier," he said quietly. "I was being an asshole."

"It's okay." I shook my head. "So was I."

He looked at me. His eyes moved from my eyes to my lips and then slowly down the length of my body.

"You wanna come inside?" he asked.

I nodded.

We went into his apartment. As he stole across the room to turn on a small lamp, I flopped onto the sofa. Suddenly nervous, I clasped my hands in my lap, trying not to let it show.

"I haven't been able to stop thinking about that scene we shot the other day," he said as he settled down beside me.

"Which scene?" I tucked a curl behind my ear, but it fell back down.

"Which scene?" he repeated.

"Yeah." I tried again to tame the errant tendril without success.

He shook his head, grinning. He reached over and secured the curl over my ear.

"You're fucking adorable, you know that?"

He let his fingers play in my hair.

"Am I?"

"Yes." He kissed my neck. With soft, tender kisses, he began to trace the lines of my neck and face.

"The scene." Kiss. "I'm talking about." Kiss. "Is the one." Kiss. "Where for the first time." Kiss.

He paused, holding my chin and looking deeply into my eyes.

"They make love."

My lips were parted and my breathing felt heavy. My whole body yearned for him—craved him. I tried to speak but it came out as more of a sigh.

"Oh yeah?" I said breathlessly.

He smiled, his wicked half-smile.

"Oh yeah," he repeated, and his mouth was on mine.

He pulled me onto his lap, the kisses uninterrupted. He ran his hands underneath my shirt, his fingertips pressing hard against my skin. When he found my nipples he twisted them with a gentle force, and I moaned. I pulled at the T-shirt he was wearing and tugged it off.

His magnificent arms, the muscles long and solid, like some sculptor's fever dream. His perfectly defined chest, with thick pecs which followed a cascade of abs to a tight waist. Those broad shoulders I had admired so often on set as he relaxed between shots, stretching out in the hot Spanish sun. Those same shoulders of my daydreams flexed and worked now as he stood from the sofa, picking me up, my legs wrapped around his midsection.

I giggled like a kid. I wasn't small and I was not used to being handled so. But he was huge and massively strong, and I felt as if I could just climb all over him. It thrilled me to be grappled with.

He carried me into the bedroom and laid me on the bed. He then proceeded to remove the remaining clothes from my body, letting his hands drag across my skin as he did. Then he undressed. He stood there, beside the bed, towering over me. Even though the room was dark, his body seemed to draw every bit of light and he glowed. It warmed my skin like sunshine.

He was fully erect and he ran his hand down the length of his shaft, letting it bounce back and slap against his stomach. Then he was on top of me, pressing his length to mine. He kissed me as his hands tangled in my curls. I ran my hands down the rippling muscles of his back. I wrapped my legs around his backside.

"Tonight," he said in a ragged whisper. "I want to take my time. And when you're ready, I want to be inside you."

I grabbed his bottom lip gently between my teeth and sucked on it.

"I'm ready now," I told him.

"You sure?"

I nodded and he lifted off me long enough to pull open the drawer of the side table. As he worked the condom on, I positioned myself farther up the bed. I lay on my stomach but felt his hands grab me, tugging me over.

"Do you mind if we do it this way?" he asked. "I want to see your face. I'll be gentle."

I willingly lay on my back and let him lift my legs to my chest. He spat into his hand and I felt his warm, wet fingers massage my hole. I breathed in deeply, willing my body to be receiving.

He inched himself in, and I fought the urge to clench. I knew, of course, how big he was, but accommodating his girth was an effort. He took his time and did not force it, and as he buried himself farther and farther, I threw my head back, a moan escaping my lips.

"Yes," he gasped.

He was fully in then, and I felt his balls gently slap on my skin. He slowly began to move his hips, taking care. And then came the moment where my body completely gave way and we coalesced. Effort turned to ecstasy and he held back no longer, passion guided his strokes, and he explored me deeply and thoroughly.

Time blurred as we bucked and rocked, switching positions, wrapping around one another. Until finally I was on my stomach again and his arms were wrapped tightly around my torso. I matched his rhythm throwing my ass back to him in counter-stroke. And then I came, hard and bright, a sunburst through my body as I soaked his sheets and myself. My body brought him to orgasm and with a final few drives, he spent himself.

He collapsed, his arms still wrapped around my chest. He wasn't ready to remove himself, and I felt him still deep inside. He kissed my shoulders and back and then nuzzled my neck.

"Oh, Xavier," he sighed, his breathing came hard and heavy like my own.

I smiled to hear my name on his lips, and I let sleep come.

• • • •

WHEN I WOKE THE NEXT morning, my arm was outstretched across where Dennis had slept. But Dennis wasn't there. His side of the bed was still warm so I rolled onto my side and pulled his pillow to me. I buried my face in it and inhaled, smelling his scent still on it. The soft drift of voices came to me from the next room.

I climbed out of bed, pulled on my underwear, and went to investigate. I found Dennis sitting at the kitchen table, in a T-shirt and boxers, a veritable grocery store spread out before him: eggs, bacon, a canister of oatmeal, a bag of oranges. But he wasn't cooking; he was talking to someone on speaker.

He hadn't noticed me, so I pulled back a little, just out of sight and leaned against the doorframe, listening.

"Oh, Xavier's great," I heard him say. "He's so good in these scenes. It really challenges me, and I love it. He's making me a better actor."

I couldn't help but grin at that.

"And he's a really cool guy. I can't wait for you to meet him."

"I'd love to," a woman's voice replied.

There was a rushing sound in my ears. Could it be? Was he really talking to Ronnie on speakerphone with me asleep in the next room? After all the drama, all the stuff he'd said when he'd been waiting for me, and now first thing he was on the phone with her? What a complete and utter fool I must've been!

"I'm glad to hear you've got a friend on set, darling," the woman continued. "I know you get real lonesome sometimes."

The river of sound in my mind snapped and dissipated. That didn't sound as if it could be Ronnie. The voice sounded much more mature and sadly strained.

"I'm okay, Mama," replied Dennis. "But how are you? What did that specialist say? Was Darlene able to get you there okay?"

"That was so sweet of you to send her money to fix her car. I can't drive those long distances anymore, and she doesn't know how to drive stick—who doesn't know how to drive stick, I ask you—so it was such a blessing for her to get her clunker going again. She said she was gonna send you a thank you card for that, but I told her to wait. Said you were over in Europe and it might never get to you. So she said she'd send it to California when you get back."

"That's fine, Mama," Dennis said a little impatiently. "I'm happy to help. But what did the specialist say?"

"Oh, doctors." His mother sighed. "All they do is try to scare you. I'm as strong as an ox, just like always. Runs in my family. My grandmama was almost a hundred when she died."

"Yes, I know."

"So I don't put no truck in what doctors have to say."

"Mama, what did he say?"

"Nothing important," she said.

"Mama," he insisted. He rubbed his neck.

"Nothing that can't wait, baby. I'm all right. He said everything is progressing well, and just to keep doing what I'm doing. Gave me a new prescription."

"What did he give you?" Dennis asked, grabbing a pen on the table.

"Oh, I can't remember the name of it. I'll look at it later and tell you."

"Make sure you do, Mama. You know I need to keep track. Just take a picture on your phone and send it to me if you want."

"I can never use this thing."

"Well, just email me then. You're good at email."

"Yes, yes, I will. But there's nothing urgent the matter right now. You just worry about doing a good job on that film and you come see me when it's all finished. And we'll catch up properly then."

"Mama, if there's something the matter—"

"Now, listen," interrupted his mother. "You heard me. We'll talk when you come to visit me. Don't you worry about me." Dennis didn't respond, just massaged his neck. "Did you hear me?"

"Yes, ma'am. I heard you."

"All right then. That's good."

"Do you need anything, Mama? Did you need any money?"

"I've still got the last you sent me, baby, and I thank you. But you don't need to waste your money on me, I'm doing okay."

"Well, it's meant to be spent. If you need anything, don't just squirrel it away in your dresser drawer."

"Do what?" His mama laughed. "I knew you used to sneak in and slip a bill or two from my mad money when you were a kid. Now you're telling on yourself."

Dennis laughed. "Only the odd five dollars or so. Do you forgive me?"

"Well, I'll think about it. So long as you hug my neck real good when I see you."

"Of course."

"Now I better go. My break's almost over. Darlene takes her meal break late so she can watch the recording of her stories from this afternoon and then give me the recap. If I don't hurry she'll be talking a hole into some poor patient's head just to tell somebody. These night shifts will drive a person batty, I swear."

"You take care of yourself. Love you, Mama."

"I love you too, Denny."

He fidgeted with the pen after disconnecting the call, tapping it against the tabletop. His head moved from side to side as if he were trying to work out a kink in his neck.

I approached slowly and put my hands on his shoulders, massaging them.

He looked up at me and smiled.

"Hey there, sleepyhead," he said.

I massaged his neck.

"Oh, that feels good," he said, closing his eyes. He let his head fall back a bit and rested it against my stomach.

"Everything okay?" I asked him.

He didn't answer for a moment.

"It's all good," he said. He opened his eyes and looked up at me. "Ready for some breakfast?"

I waved my hand over all the choices on the table.

"Did you raid the local store?" I asked with a laugh.

"I just wanted to be prepared," he said with a wink as he stood. "Besides our call time isn't until late this afternoon."

"Yeah, so?"

He pulled me to him, wrapping his arms around my waist.

"So I need you to get fueled up," he said. "Stockpile energy."

He kissed my neck.

"For the shoot?" I asked.

"Nope," he said, kissing up the line of my neck and grazing my jawline with his teeth. "For round two."

He pulled my mouth to his and kissed me deeply.

"Now, decide what you want to eat," he said. "I'm gonna go shower."

As he passed me, he smacked my ass.

The sun god himself was going to cook me breakfast. If I smiled any harder, I was afraid my jaw would pop loose. This was too good to be true.

I glanced at the cell phone he'd left on the table, its screen black.

Let's hope not, I said to myself.

CHAPTER TEN

"**A**re you lying to me?"
       "*No*," I declared.
"Are you lying to yourself maybe?"
"What is that supposed to mean?" I snapped.

Marisa Guadel, who played my aunt in this scene, walked over to the table and mashed her cigarette onto the plate near my arm. I was seated just outside the hotel location, at a small table, a drinking glass and the small plate covering it. She adjusted the bright auburn wig she wore as it said in the script.

"Then tell me where you were last night," she said.

"I already told you, tía, I was out with Cecilia and some friends."

"Ya basta! Todas la mentiras – you were not with Cecilia last night, I know this. She came looking for you this morning, while you were still asleep, to ask if you were okay. She has not seen you in three days, she said. Do not lie to me."

"Why do I owe you an explanation?"

"Because this is my home! You are my responsibility while you are here! Of course, you owe me an explanation."

"You don't understand anyway."

"I do not understand what? Dime. What is so hard to tell your aunt? What could you have done in one night?"

I got up from the table and went to lean against the nearby wall.

"A lot can change in one night. Whole lives. What if I woke up an entirely different person than I went to sleep as?"

"What are you talking about? You are the same boy I knew yesterday."

"Am I? I'm not sure, tía."

"What does this have to do with where you were?"

"Everything, tía. Everything! If I tell you where I was—what I was doing—who I was doing it with—then you will not want to hear it. You will not see me as the same boy you knew yesterday."

"¡Qué disparates estás diciendo!"

"It's not nonsense at all. I have changed. And maybe the way you see me will change."

"What could be so wrong?"

"What if you love me differently, tía? Maybe you don't deserve an explanation because you will love me differently. And if you can't know me as I am—as I am changed—maybe you do not deserve to love me. What if...?"

I faltered. Hot tears had begun streaming down my face. This was not the way we'd rehearsed it; this was not how I planned to play out the scene. But still, they came. In a rush, a great flood of tears."

"What if...?"

I tried to say my line but it would not come. Marisa extemporized.

"What are you trying to tell me, *mi amor?*"

I looked up at her, my face wet.

"I don't know," I cried. "I don't know."

A great pain, like a suppressed howl of sorrow, engulfed my chest. I gasped, trying to catch my breath, the sobs coming in gulps. I ran forward then, I couldn't say why. It was not written in the scene, not at all how it was meant to be. But I ran forward and threw my arms around Marisa, clutching onto her.

Something broke within me, like a great dam opening to a waterfall, and I began to weep, my face buried in her chest. Marisa pulled me to her, her arms around me, going with it.

"*Ay, cariño mío*, tell to your aunt what is so wrong?"

I tried to speak but the words choked in my mouth. They came out a garbled sob. I couldn't say what I was supposed to; the lines of script jumbled in my mind until everything was static. The sobs wracked me and I couldn't stop the tears.

Marisa just stroked my hair and leaned back against the wall, holding me. She hummed a little melody, rocking me as she did until my breathing evened out and I finally got ahold of myself.

I pulled away from her slightly, lifting my head.

"I'm sorry," I said quietly.

She stroked my cheek, saying nothing, but smiling with warmth and understanding.

Softly from somewhere nearby I heard Carlos say, "Cut."

I looked at Marisa in astonishment and she just smiled and ruffled my hair. I covered my face with my hands, mortified at how I had lost control.

Carlos rushed forward and put his arm over my shoulders, leading me to the side.

"Carlos, I'm so, so sorry." My voice was heavy with embarrassment. "That was a complete mess. I'm so sorry. I don't know what came over—"

"Sorry?" Carlos exclaimed. "*Mi amor*, nonsense! Who cares about the words I wrote. They are irrelevant. That was much better than I could have ever written. Everything was communicated. It said everything."

"A-a-are you sure?" I asked, slightly baffled.

"It was perfect, I assure you. Perfect!" He put his hands on my shoulders. "But I think that is enough for today, yes? Tomorrow we have a rest day—no scenes for you. Tonight you rest, have a little wine. What is it you Americans love to say? Self-care? You take this."

"But—"

"No, no, no but. I am so happy. But I want you to be fresh. A new scene in a couple of days. Go, go. Enjoy these last days."

These last days? Oh, god, he was right. I hadn't let myself process the fact that we only had a few more scenes to shoot and then it was over. All over.

I nodded and took the handkerchief he offered to clean myself up. I shook my head in disbelief. The summer was coming to an end. It wasn't something I wanted to think about right now, not something I *could* think about. I shook my head and pushed all those thoughts away.

Now, I would head to Glamor Central and get out of wardrobe. That was all I could think about. As I headed off, I noticed Dennis was standing just off set, near the monitor. He had seen the whole scene. What did he think? He was staring at me now, studying. I saw him lift his hand as if to wave, but I turned my head sharply and trotted off.

I prayed for rain. The endless, dry, overheated days had been going on for weeks. It was overwhelming. Just a bit of relief, some release, a gasp of air, anything to conquer the relentlessness. I wasn't sure how much longer I could take this.

• • • •

I AWOKE TO KNOCKING at my door. I was groggy, my vision blurry. I had taken Carlos's advice and drank some wine, and then had a long, hot bath, and maybe a sleeping pill. I was so done in that I had apparently fallen asleep on top of the made bed, still in my bathrobe. I reluctantly pushed myself up from the mattress and stumbled to the front salon of my flat.

The knocking continued even though I did not call out or acknowledge. It was not loud, but persistent. I wondered how long he—whoever it was—had been standing there, rapping their knuckles.

"Hey, buddy," said Dennis as I opened the door. "What you up to, sleepyhead?"

"Hey, Dennis," I mumbled.

"Everything okay?" he asked. His smile was bright, but he looked worried.

I nodded.

"It's just I stopped by last night, and you didn't answer the door. And then you didn't answer your cell or any of my texts. I just wanted to make sure everything was okay."

"I'm okay," I replied.

"You sure?" he asked. "Yesterday was a lot—that scene—it was really powerful. It must have taken a lot out of you."

"Yeah, it did. Guess I just needed to disconnect for a bit, you know."

"Sure." He took a hesitant step forward. "Okay if I come in?"

I leaned against the door, hesitant.

"Umm, I don't know."

His eyes flashed and the lines around them crinkled as he squinted, trying to stave off some emotion.

"Did I do something, Zay?" he asked softly. "Because if I made you angry or anything…"

The look on his face pained me. I wanted to shut the door; I wanted to push him back down the front walk and lock the gate. I wanted him to come inside, untie my robe, and kiss me, naked, in the sunlight streaming through the front windows.

I shook my head.

"You're not the problem, Denny. I'm the problem."

"What?" he asked, confused.

"Nothing," I said.

He glanced over his shoulder nervously.

"It's just that I got these two rental Vespas. And I figured, you know, we have the day off and everything. I've got some *queso manchego*, *berenjenas*, and white wine. All your local favorites," he smiled and raised his eyebrows.

God, he can be so corny sometimes, I thought. I resisted the urge to roll my eyes.

"I thought maybe we could go up into the mountains. There's supposed to be some killer spots there that we haven't seen yet. Really isolated and beautiful. If you're up for it? We don't even have to talk if you don't want to. Just ride. And maybe take a hike. Or swim?"

Cocking his head to the side, he let his eyes slowly and obviously trace the length of my body as he mentioned swimming.

God, I hate him, I told myself. I couldn't believe how just one look from him, even when I wanted to slam the door in his face, made me feel like putty, just waiting to be manhandled.

He paused and looked at me expectantly. I didn't respond.

"No pressure," he insisted. "Let's get lost for a little bit."

I closed my eyes and inhaled deeply, taking a deep steadying breath. I could smell him when I did, and the warmth of the day beyond, and it filled my body.

"Okay," I said, opening my eyes. "Let's get lost."

He broke into a smile so radiant I couldn't help but smile back.

* * * *

I OPENED MY EYES TO the night. The stars shone above and I stretched my arms out in the grass, liking the feel of moonlight on my naked body. Dennis murmured in his sleep. I lay there for a moment, listening to the sound of the lapping water.

We had managed to find a spot of green, high up in the mountains that surrounded the village. A small grove of trees lay just behind the large rough outcroppings of rock that speared up from the ground in this part of the range. They bordered a small lake of sorts—a perfect place to swim and not be noticed. After our small but delicious picnic—he really had gathered all of my favorite things from the village—we had decided to strip down to our underwear and swim in the unexpectedly cold water, shivering and laughing. We splashed around like school kids, pushing one another under the surface, tackling each other and wrestling, until finally, we tumbled onto the dry grass under the trees.

That morning I'd sworn to myself that I was going to end this, that I needed to get this whole stupid affair out of my system. I was barreling toward a terrible end, and I needed to swerve away from the wall I knew was approaching to avoid a terrible crash. But there, by the water, hidden away from the rest of the world, just the two of us, my resolve faltered and my body gave in. I made love with abandon, letting myself believe, if only for these moments, that it could always be like this.

Seeing Denny lying there now, the twilight glinting off his dewy wet body, boxer shorts clinging to his skin, I wanted to believe it still. The sun god himself, now the god of moonlight as well. I wanted him all ways, all times. The crash was inevitable; I couldn't turn away and I hated myself for it.

Dennis stirred. He turned onto his side, the arm he had lifted over his eyes to block out the sunlight falling to his side. He blinked and looked up at me staring down at him.

"What?" he asked with a crooked smile.

I smiled and shook my head. "Nothing."

I leaned over and kissed him.

It felt like something out of a movie. *But then, it is, isn't it?* I thought to myself. This whole thing, secluded in this picturesque place, all of our attention devoted to telling a love story, devoted to one another, our own little world. Sometimes it seemed unreal.

I shook my head and wondered how late it was. I remembered that I couldn't check because our cell phones were back in the village. Just as we were leaving, he had gotten a phone call that made his jaw tense as he pushed the red button to ignore. I couldn't see the screen, but I could only guess. Then he was suddenly struck with the idea to leave our electronics behind.

Let's just enjoy the peace, he'd said. *Let's get lost.*

Get lost. Run away. If only we could. If only this little world was real and not some insect caught in amber. Beautiful, fascinating, but utterly detached from real life.

"What time is it?" he asked.

"I don't know," I said sharply.

"It's gotten dark. Look at all those stars."

"Yeah." I turned away, biting my lip, feeling a sudden rush of emotion I couldn't completely understand.

"Is this how it always is?" I suddenly blurted out. "Is this what you do with all your costars?"

"What?" he said, confused, frowning.

"Seduce them and keep them in your sway with lovemaking sessions under the stars?"

He sat up and looked at me. He could see my ire was up and he tried to ease the tension.

He ran his finger down my arm.

"I'm entirely sure we can say who seduced who here."

I brushed his hand away.

"I'm for real, Denny. Is that why you took this film? So you can have some secret escape and sexcapades for a few weeks and then back to the picture-perfect Hollywood life?"

"Hey, slow down. Where is all this coming from? I thought we had a nice afternoon. Why are you suddenly so bent out of shape?"

I glared at him. I shook my head, refusing to change course.

"For one thing," he said. "This just happened—you and I, I mean. There was no scheming. I didn't even know who I'd be working with, much less if they'd be amenable to man-on-man action. Or whatever machinations you think me capable of."

"Oh please. You're a fucking gorgeous and charming movie star. You think anyone could resist you?"

"Thanks for the compliment, I suppose," he said, his voice heavy with sarcasm. "But it's not like I'm walking around thinking of who I am going to hypnotize with my fame. It means a lot more to other people than it does to me. Is that the only reason you're attracted to me?"

"Of course not. That's not what I meant, and you know it. It's just— Fuck. I just feel foolish."

"I know it's fucked-up. Believe me, I do. And, no, I didn't take this job so I could get my kicks. Despite what you might think I don't go around fucking every willing accomplice. I'm not the type of person. In fact, this is the first time I've even indulged in this... this kind of thing since... well, since the engagement."

I wasn't sure I believed that.

"So why now?"

He only looked at me then. His jaw worked but he didn't speak, it was as if he couldn't bring himself to make the words real.

"Don't you see this isn't fair?" I asked him. "To either me or Ronnie. I chose this. I am participating with full knowledge. So I'm an asshole too, I guess. And whatever karma I get, I deserve. But this just isn't the way. In the end, there's going to be two people hurting."

He turned away, resting his head against his knees.

"You're wrong, you know," he said. "There's gonna be three people hurting."

I looked at him, the moonlight across his bare back, and my heart ached for him. It felt as if it might crack in two. I knew he didn't mean to hurt anybody. I knew he was confused, conflicted. But it still didn't change the truth of what we were doing, the betrayal we were engaging in. And even as I admitted that to myself, all I wanted to do was hold him, pull him close, and assure him it was all right.

I laid my hand against his back. I felt the muscles tense up and then slowly relax.

"Maybe we should head back," I said after a long pause.

He shook his head.

"You go back; I'm gonna go for a walk."

"But we're miles from the village. And it's pitch black up here."

He stood, pulling on his shorts, and grabbing his shirt and shoes.

"It's fine. I could use some time to think. Maybe I just need to disconnect too. You know?"

Stung, I didn't reply.

As I rode back to the village, I couldn't keep anything straight and I felt as if I were somehow losing grip on reality. I knew I was definitely coming off as hot and cold in a dizzying fashion. But I couldn't make it fit. I wanted him so badly and yet I knew it was headed for a wall. I prayed the next few days would go quickly and at the same time, I prayed they would never end. I had to be the one to put a stop to this.

But even as I pulled up to my place, I knew I couldn't. I grabbed my bag from the back of the bike and stood staring across the street at his flat. I knew it was empty; I knew he was miles away still. But I stood there; imagining that a light would turn on and he would saunter out to the patio and invite me inside.

I knew that was all I wanted in that moment.

I knew I didn't have the strength to end it then.

I knew I was doomed.

CHAPTER ELEVEN

"**C**ut!"

Carlos twirled his hand in the air. "Let's do that one once more, please."

He walked over to us.

"Xavier, do you want to take a break?" he asked me in a thoughtful tone.

"No, I'm fine. Let's try another take."

"Are you sure?"

"Yeah, yeah. Totally."

But I wasn't sure. This was already the fourth take I'd screwed up, and my anxiety was building. Dennis was studying me, silently.

"A break might be good," he finally said.

"No," I said. "I'm fine. Let's just get it done."

He made a face and shrugged, turning away from me.

It was our last scene together. We each had a few more scenes to shoot with other actors, and a few pick-up shots, but this would be the last time we were on set together. And Carlos had purposely saved it until the end of the shoot. It was a big moment in the script; the scene where the two characters finally confess their love. There was supposed to be this discussion of their plans, and a stunning, beautiful, heartfelt kiss that encapsulated the breadth of their love and passion for one another. At least, that's how it read in the script. But every time we tried to play the scene, I choked. I fumbled and lost my place or, when I actually remembered the lines, I delivered them either completely woodenly or with shiver-inducing over-the-top melodrama. It was just too much.

In less than a week, we'd be packing up the equipment and getting on planes to go our separate ways. The film would be in the can. We'd be leaving La Mancha. Neither of us had broached the subject—it seemed, in fact, that we were pointedly ignoring it.

It didn't help my muddled mind that Denny was now playing this scene with all the tenderness, and then some, that it required. If he was an emotional shipwreck inside, as I was, it certainly wasn't showing on the outside. Every time he touched me, every time he looked into my eyes and delivered a line, another wave of emotion battered my chest, threatening to capsize me.

"Are we ready?" asked Carlos.

Denny and I both nodded.

"Can we take it from the first kiss then?" Carlos suggested. "By the window. Just before the main dialogue starts."

As Carlos called for quiet, I took my place on the windowsill. As my character sat peering out of the window, Denny's character was meant to approach and kiss me. Denny took his mark, a few feet away. We exchanged glances.

"Okay?" he whispered.

I nodded.

Someone clapped the sticks and Carlos signaled for action.

Dennis approached me. There was an HMI light just out of shot meant to mimic the sunlight through the window and as he stepped forward, it fell onto him. It caught his skin, the highlights of his hair, everything about him seemed to glow. It called to mind the first moments when I'd seen him in the hotel lobby—could it have only been three months ago? He emanated light, warmth. I wanted it to envelop me, to drown me in the glow, to suffocate me in the very essence of him.

He was in front of me and I looked up at him in awe. He ran his hands along my thighs and tilted his head, his gaze tracing the lines of my face.

"I've been looking for you," he said.

It was his scripted line. Something inside me, some crystalline thread that had been spun from the light he emanated, cracked again. It was his line—his line—and I knew what my next line was supposed to be. It wasn't Dennis speaking; it was his character. Suddenly his hands felt cold against my skin. The lights seemed to dim. I spoke my next words, almost robotically. My body felt rigid.

He leaned in to kiss me, as was written, and his lips connected with mine. I felt myself kiss him back and suddenly I wanted to pull away. It felt like a mockery, like a taunting, and my head reared back slightly.

No, I chastised myself, *do your damn job, man. This is why you're here.* I pushed forward then, back into the kiss, catching Dennis slightly off guard. Our noses smashed together and I moved with a jerk trying to correct our path. My teeth came down and I tasted something salty on my tongue. Dennis snapped his head back and his hand flew to his mouth.

"I think you bit my lip," he said in quiet surprise.

"Oh, fuck, Dennis, I'm sorry," I moaned.

"Cut!" I heard Carlos cry once again.

I ran my hands down my face, muttering apologies.

The anger and frustration I had for myself boiled up inside me and I threw my hands back from my face as I roared,

"Fuck!" I felt my elbow connect with the windowpane behind me and heard the shatter.

"Zay!" Denny exclaimed as he started forward.

He grabbed me by the waist and scooted me forward on the sill as I pulled my elbow around to examine it.

"Are you okay?" he asked.

No blood, not even a scratch, we both saw.

"I guess I'm fine," I said, stunned.

"Can't say the same for that window," Denny said flatly and we both burst out laughing.

"Come on," he said, giving me his arm. "Let's get you away from that broken glass before Carlos has a heart attack."

"Too late, *mi amor*," said Carlos, who had come up behind. "I have had at least three and now I am on the verge of the nervous breakdown."

"Sorry, Carlos," I said, much chagrinned.

"It's fine, it's fine. It is only a piece of glass. Thank god you are not injured." He took my hand and kissed it, making me smile. "For one thing, we cannot afford the insurance if our lead actor is bleeding all over the set, no?"

He turned to the crew.

"Okay, everybody. We clean this up and get new glass and then we set up again after lunch, *sí*?" The crew grumbled their assent and he turned to me. "Can the two of you meet me in my office in about ten minutes?"

"Of course," I replied.

Dennis and I exchanged silent grimaces.

• • • •

TEN MINUTES LATER AS requested, we walked into the downstairs study that served as Carlos's temporary office. He was standing by the window, looking over the shooting script, and when we entered he motioned for us to sit in two chairs that were facing each other.

"Look, Carlos, I know I've been fucking up, but I swear I can—"

"Ah, ah, ah," he interrupted. "No apologies, *cariño*. That's not why I asked you here. Just listen, please."

He crossed the room so that he was behind me. I heard a soft *click* and suddenly the room filled with music.

Dennis smiled at the familiar beat, and I couldn't help but smile too.

"You remember this song, eh?" said Carlos, crossing back to the window. "This is the song that I wanted to use for your first kiss scene. I think you liked it too, no? Maybe we just close our eyes and listen to it now."

Carlos leaned against the wall and closed his eyes, and I followed suit. I listened as the lyrics began, remembering that first time we did kiss. Not on-set, as Carlos had mentioned, but when we'd first *really* kissed, the two of us alone in my apartment. Denny's warm body pressed to mine, his hand on my thigh.

I was lost / When I first tasted your lips
My head spun / When my hands gripped your hips

I opened my eyes and found Dennis staring at me. His eyes shone bright, swirling with emotion, as if he wanted to say something but couldn't find the words. I lifted my chin, prompting him to speak. His lips parted but he remained silent. He sighed, looking down and then back up at me. There was something in his expression that I read as sadness. He gave me a meek shrug. I nodded.

We sat for a while as the music played just staring at one another. The last bridge of the song built, and I could feel the singer's voice in my chest as he sang:

Oh, it's not like I ever thought I had it all figured out
But seeing your face has me filled with such doubt
I'm questioning all the things I ever knew about me
Yeah, that man's a stranger, oh, who is he

My breath caught and my chest felt tight. I turned my head, looking away from Dennis. I closed my eyes.

"There," said Carlos, softly, as the song faded out. "That puts us back in the place, no? We are in our minds back in the time of the characters, what they were feeling. Was that any help?"

I nodded.

"Yes," I heard Denny reply but I kept my focus on Carlo. "Thank you."

"You're welcome," Carlos answered, holding my gaze solidly.

"So," he continued. "Now we have lunch. And then we meet back on set. With a new outlook. And a new window. *Ojalá.*"

I stood up.

"I'll meet you guys on set," I said, moving swiftly to the door. "I'm gonna go for a short walk."

• • • •

REALIZING THAT WITH the time difference Jaelyn would still be asleep, I decided to simply wander. Headphones in my ears and the song *Goner* on repeat. I strolled to the *Cuadrado de María* and back. I tried to do all I could to push all the conflicting ideas out of my head, to draw a veil over my own emotions and get inside the fictional mind of my character.

I stopped by Glamor Central for a fresh outfit and then headed to set. I was waiting by the window when the crew returned from lunch.

"Try not to break this one, eh, *niño*?" said one of the grips as he passed me.

Yeah, Zay, try not to fuck it up this time, I told myself as I settled onto the windowsill.

"All good?" Denny asked as he took his mark again.

"All good."

"One moment," announced Carlos. "Nobody move. Give me one second."

He trotted out of the room with the AD.

Denny sauntered over and leaned against the windowsill as we waited. He gave me one of his crooked smiles and I felt light dance in my chest.

"Now, remember, if you get frustrated this time, punch forward, not back," he teased.

"Then I'd end up punching you," I said.

He shrugged. "I'm tough, I can take a hit."

"Just as long as you don't punch me back. I'm not as tough as you."

He let his arm fall at his side and moved the back his hand along the ledge of the window. His knuckles danced lightly across my fingers.

"I don't know about that, Zay. I think you're much stronger than you give yourself credit for," he said quietly.

His hand was on top of mine, and it was all I could see. I felt mute, unable to speak.

"Okay, okay," called Carlos from across the room. "Sorry about that. Everything is okay. Places, please."

Dennis gave me a light, playful punch on the shoulder.

"Okay, buddy," he said. "Let's do this."

"Sure thing, Jimmy," I replied, remembering the joke from our first meeting.

He let out a guffaw and moved back to his mark. When he turned to me, his eyes sparkled with mirth.

This moment. This is what I wanted to keep. To freeze it exactly as it was and lock it away like some treasure. Some beloved artifact, more like. This moment would dissolve very soon and be no more. I was determined to hold onto it now though, capture it for just a tiny bit longer.

"Action," called Carlos and we began the scene.

"*I've been looking for you*," Dennis repeated his line, his hands on my waist.

I lifted my hand and caressed his neck. I felt the *click* in me and I was in the moment.

"*You know I'm never far from you.*"

He leaned in for a kiss and our lips met. I ran my hand through his hair, pulling him closer.

I slipped my hand under his shirt and rubbed that spot in the small of his back that I knew drove him crazy. Him, Dennis, the real man not the character. He moaned ever so slightly and his kiss deepened. I wrapped my legs around his. The world disappeared. The lights, the camera, the crew watching all disappeared. I closed my eyes and the heat on my skin felt like sunshine. I knew this scent, his scent, and I inhaled, breathed deeply of it. It was mine; it didn't belong to anyone else, to any other world but my own at this moment. I felt the sunshine explode inside and I let it move through me and into him.

He broke away, breathless, resting his forehead against mine. He met my eyes, his expression slightly dazed.

Even so, he remembered his line.

"I'll remember this summer forever."

Another *click* inside me.

It cut too close to the quick. The sunshine turned to fire.

"I don't believe you," I said. "You won't remember."

Just a flicker in his eyes. These were my words, not some script. He knew and he went with it.

"Do you think I could ever forget you?"

"Yes. Easily."

"I won't. I can't. I promise you."

"What do your promises mean? When we leave, when we're back there, it won't be any different."

He took my face in his hands.

"I'll make it different," his voice was grave, desperate. "I swear to you. It's a promise."

He kissed me again, hard, urgently.

I broke away.

"I don't want promises," I said, my heart in my throat. "I just want this."

He traced his finger along the curve of my bottom lip, nodding.

"And cut!"

Carlos's voice was like a smack in the face.

I blinked and looked over to see the DP crouched beside us, camera rig on his shoulder. He stood, stretching his back, giving Carlos a thumbs-up.

I shook my head, trying to clear it. Denny turned away, hand to his forehead.

"Sorry, we can do it again," he said.

"What do you talk about?" exclaimed Carlos. "You are crazy. That was *perfecto*. *Lo maximo*. We have plenty of coverage we can cut from the other takes, but I won't need it."

"But we went completely off-script," I exclaimed.

"I don't care about words, *mijo*. I care about feelings. *La evocación, sí?* I care about the truth. Only the truth. *La verdad, coño!*"

Standing between us, he rested a hand on each of our shoulders.

"I wrote the words, *claro*, but you made it the truth. I don't want to ruin it with too much acting, *me entiendes*? I don't need it to be too much of a movie. I need it to be what it is."

A storm of confusion raged inside me and I tried to still it with a deep breath.

"Okay," I conceded.

"So we're done then?" asked Denny, a little too casually.

"Yes," said Carlos and he turned around, signaling to the crew to begin packing up.

I willed my feet to move, although they felt made of stone, and headed toward the door.

Dennis was behind me and laid his hand on my shoulder.

"You okay, man?" he asked.

I shrugged off his grip.

"I'm fine," I said and quickly left the room.

I was down the stairs and moving up the sidewalk when I heard his voice.

"Hey, Zay," Dennis called. "Zay, man, what's the rush?"

I kept walking without pause.

"Zay, come on. Can you just wait a second? Xavier!"

"What?" I snapped, whirling around.

My expression must have been as fierce as my reply because he took a step back.

"Are you sure you're okay?"

I felt a tightness in my throat. I swallowed hard against the threat of tears I felt in my eyes. *No, no, no,* I wanted to bellow. *Of course, I'm not all right! I'm losing you! This is it. It's over.*

"I said I'm fine."

He gave me a look. "Well, it's just... I don't know. This is our last scene together. And I just thought maybe, you know..."

"Thought what, Dennis?"

He looked defeated. He shrugged, running his hands across his face and letting them fall lamely at his side.

"I don't know, man. I don't know what I thought."

I nodded and turned away, starting off again, slowly.

"Hey, Zay," he called out quietly.

"Yeah?" I paused.

"I'll see you at the wrap party though, right?"

I sighed.

"Yes. Of course."

I headed off in the direction of my flat. At first, I moved slowly but then I picked up the pace and before I knew it I was running as hard as I could. My legs were pumping, hurtling me away from everything behind. I pushed and pushed, hoping that once I reached home I could throw myself into bed, exhausted, and melt into the black oblivion of sleep.

CHAPTER TWELVE

S *even months later.*
New York City.

• • • •

AFTER THE SHOW, I HUNG out in my dressing room until I was sure most of the rest of the cast had left. Tonight had been a good performance, finally; one I could be proud of. I knew everyone was especially pleased, but somehow having to hear congratulations seemed more imposing than getting everyone's cold shoulders. So I hid out.

Despite the fact that the run had ended up going smoothly, I was only just feeling in my usual groove. Even so, I was glad this play was a limited engagement. On the other hand, I didn't have anything immediately lined up—no work to throw myself into—except for the upcoming press junket. But I tried to push thoughts of that out of my mind.

I was nodding my goodbye to our doorman when I heard someone calling my name from the near-empty wings and I cringed.

"Hey, Xavier, I thought you'd left," said Andrew, our director.

"Not yet," I answered sheepishly.

"I just wanted to say thanks for tonight," he said, approaching. "We haven't really talked about things since rehearsals. That was a rough spot, I know, so I didn't want to harp on it. But whatever it was that had you so blocked, you soldiered through. And, frankly, I'm floored at how you've turned it around. I'll admit I was worried about you for a bit. I wondered if they'd sent me a different actor than the one I'd auditioned. You really had me quaking in my boots."

I nodded. "Yeah, sorry about that."

"I won't pry," said Andrew. "But I hope you're doing better now. And, again, thanks for whatever voodoo you worked because you've been amazing. I don't have to hide my face from anybody or change my name after all."

He laughed loudly and I gave a tight smile.

"Sorry, hope that doesn't sound completely self-centered," he added, clapping me on the shoulder.

"Not at all," I said, proving again that I was a good actor.

"We're gonna give them a closing weekend for the books."

"You bet," I said. Saved by the bell, I thought as my cell started to ring. "Sorry, I've gotta take this."

"Of course. See you tomorrow," replied Andrew as I dashed out of the stage door.

I bounded onto the street, wrapping my scarf tighter around my neck as I answered the call.

"Biiiiitch! Why didn't you tell me the poster was out today!"

"Hey, Jaelyn," I answered with a chuckle.

"Oh my god, it is everything! Don't tell me you haven't seen it yet."

"I haven't actually," I lied.

Of course, I'd seen the picture. I spent most of my free time stalking Denny on social media. Not that there was much to see, mostly movie star stuff, related to his new project—the action flick he'd secured in London. Him on location in some exotic place; him smiling in a group photo; him with his arm around his stunt double.

"Dennis and Carlos both posted it earlier, along with some behind-the-scenes shots. You guys look adorable. I'm surprised you didn't get them."

"I've been off social media for a few days. I've been kinda keeping to myself lately."

"Yeah, I've *been kinda* noticing that."

"Sorry."

"No apologies, babe. But you know I'm here whenever you want to talk?"

"Yeah, I know."

"Good. Cuz I am going to be calling your ass constantly. Because I am flipping out and this isn't even my movie. Are you living or what?"

I started laughing; Jaelyn's enthusiasm was always infectious and always a tonic.

"When is the premiere?" she said.

"I'm not sure if we're doing LA or NYC first, I have to check. We have a few festival screenings before then, anyway."

"'But you're obviously invited as my date to whichever premiere comes first, Jaelyn.' You meant to say?"

"Obviously."

"Good. I can feel it on this one, babe. The studio is really pushing it. I've heard all kinds of stuff around town, even the words Oscar buzz and it hasn't even screened yet. You and Dennis are going to get so much attention."

"Yeah, it's pretty exciting," I said flatly.

"Well, that was completely convincing," she said with sarcasm.

"I'm just tired, I guess. It hasn't really hit me yet. And I'm still kinda wrapped in the headspace of this play and all that."

"Of course," she agreed but I could tell she wasn't buying it. "Dennis seems pretty excited about it too."

I stopped midstride. A pedestrian bumped into me, muttering, "Get off the sidewalk, asshole."

"So you spoke to Dennis?" I asked, trying to keep my tone measured.

"Well, I couldn't very well attend the man's birthday party and not speak to him. It was this past weekend, remember? We texted about it before."

"Yeah, guess I just lost track of the days," I said. "How was he doing?"

"To be completely honest, he looked really crestfallen when he saw me. I think he only really invited me on the off chance that you'd come with me."

"Of course not. He loved you. And he knows I'm in a play."

"Yes, I did remind him that you were on the complete opposite coast right now. It was cute, he kind of blushed. But, anyway, all he talked about was you."

I grimaced. "Oh, come on, Jae."

"Bitch, I do not lie. He played the good host or whatever, but every time he made his way back to me, which—listen—was a few too many times, the conversation made its way back to you. The man was digging for information harder than a broke archaeologist looking for treasure."

I chuckled. "Oh, whatever. You're so silly."

"Whatever nothing. That cold shoulder routine you're pulling is working, baby, he is so thirsty."

"It's not a routine."

Jaelyn sucked in air through her teeth.

"Baby, you completely cut him off. Like, full-stop, period, end of sentence, send no further telegrams."

"I didn't cut him off. I just separated myself from a bad situation. Which was bad, I may remind you, because of all of his stuff, not because I wanted to."

"If you say so, sis. But tell me you weren't hoping it would work like this."

I scoffed even though the truth was hard to deny.

"Anyway, if his feelings are hurt, he's got his beautiful fiancée to make him feel better."

"Or not. She certainly wasn't anywhere nearby during the party."

"What? Are you sure?"

"I mean, he didn't change his status from It's Complicated to Single but he was most definitely alone."

"But wasn't it at their place?"

"I suppose to. But I certainly didn't see any signs of it being *their* place. Looked like a single occupant home to me. At least from snooping around when no one was looking. And you know I'm good at snooping."

"You are the most, Jae."

"The absolute most."

I suddenly felt exhausted and weighed down.

"I better go," I said. "It's freezing out here. I'll call you tomorrow?"

"You better."

"I miss you like crazy, can't wait to see you soon."

"Ditto, obviously, bitch," she replied and paused. "But, for real, this film is going to be really great, Zay. I feel it. Don't let any of that other shit get in the way, okay? You should enjoy your moment. You deserve it."

"I will, I promise."

"Okay, goodnight, babe."

I leaned against the side of a building, lost in thought. So Dennis had been asking about me? Maybe I should have answered his invitation after all, instead of ignoring it. At least to wish him a happy birthday. But I just assumed it was a generic group text. Or had I just told myself that? I wouldn't have known what to say if the text had led to a phone call or anything else. That was the real reason I didn't respond—I was too scared of more.

I zipped my jacket up tighter, inhaling deeply of the cold night air, and trundled off to find the subway entrance.

• • • •

AS I ENTERED MY APARTMENT, my phone began to ring again. I slammed the door shut and answered.

"Xavier!" My agent, Evan, thundered in his too-deep baritone. "Zay, good baby, man, I hear you were on fucking fire tonight!"

"Thanks, Evan. Glad to hear it."

"Not half as glad as me, pal! Not gonna lie to you, my man, but we were all worried. That dress rehearsal, my god what a catastrophe. We were seriously worried you'd lost the touch there for a minute! But not for nothing, you burned that stage to bits opening night. And you've just kept on burning."

"I know," I replied, chewing on my bottom lip. "It's just that I've been in a weird headspace I guess—"

"Pal, friend, don't explain," Evan interrupted. "Don't worry about it. Everyone has their process, you know? What matters is you got there in the end. You got asses in the seats and good reviews in the rags. And you've got the festival in two weeks. We're really excited about this film."

"Yeah, the festival."

"Did you see the poster James Dennis posted?"

"Not yet. I heard about it."

"Yeah, yeah. Great pictures—you two look terrific. He's got a ton of likes already. Check your email—you've got a few to choose from. Make sure you spread them around on social media. Build the hype. The film is already getting a lot of buzz, the studio is ready to really push it, so you got to be on your A-game. Gonna be a long press junket. This festival is just the first stop. You're gonna be traveling the fucking world, my man, for at least a solid two, three months. Take your vitamins, kid."

He laughed his rough laugh.

"All right, kid, you let me know if you need anything. And I'll see you closing night. My man!"

"Thanks, Evan."

"Hey, that's what I'm here for, right? And post those pictures—build the hype!"

"Got it, yeah. 'Build the hype.'"

I resisted the urge to look at the publicity photos. I wasn't sure what seeing his face would do to me right now. Not tonight. But I felt guilty about how I'd been behaving so I quickly texted him belated birthday wishes. I lay back, closing my eyes. As I drifted to sleep, I told myself not to dream about him, but secretly hoped I would.

• • • •

THE PHONE BUZZED AND my eyes shot open. I didn't know what time it was, but sunlight was streaming through my window. I grappled around on the bed, trying to find the cell. I snatched it up, hoping to see his name.

It was a series of text messages from Liberto.

I smacked myself, feeling like a fool for how desperately I had wanted it to be Dennis.

> **[LIBERTO]**
> **Hey, papo, I have tickets to your show**
> **I get in tomorrow for 3 days**
> **Wanna go for a drink – or whatever - after the show?**

I dropped the phone onto my pillow.

I shook my head and silently chastised myself. What the fuck was wrong with me? I was pining over some closet case who was on the other side of the country. Meanwhile, a man—a sexy-ass, decidedly-into-me man—was buying tickets to come see my show and wanted to spend the evening with me.

Was I a complete fool?

No, I decided I wasn't. I grabbed the phone and texted Liberto back without waiting.

I was definitely down for drinks. Or whatever.

CHAPTER THIRTEEN

I was getting a little tipsy. I blamed it on the fact that I never ate before a show, and I'd had quite a few drinks since we arrived at the bar. But, too, I wondered if part of my giddiness was Liberto himself. He was as handsome, perhaps even more so than I remembered. And the last few months I had lived like a monk, cutting myself off from anything emotional or physical that even hinted at romance or lust.

And here I was with this sexy man who was focusing all his attention on me. From the second I'd walked out of the stage door, he swooped me up in a big hug and showered me with compliments on my performance. It felt good to feel male attention, male affection. It felt good to feel wanted again.

Maybe I was really—finally—moving on.

"So you ready for this press tour?" he asked me.

"I think so. It's my first really big one. I'm excited but a little intimidated. I hope I don't wreck it. But I'll be glad to see everybody again."

"So Dennis is doing it?"

"What do you mean? Why wouldn't he?"

"Oh, I just heard through the grapevine that he was thinking of skipping the European leg of the junket and just doing a few here in LA and NYC."

"That's odd. Did they say why?"

Liberto shrugged.

"That'd be a major loss wouldn't it?" I continued. "I mean since he's the name in the cast, the big movie star."

Liberto looked at me.

130

"Yeah, but I don't think it'd be a loss really. They'd still have you as the main attraction."

I shook my head.

"I'm terrible at interviews. I get all tongue-tied and just sound goofy."

He reached over and tucked a fallen curl behind my ear.

"A little bit, yeah." He laughed at my guffaw. "But it's endearing as hell. And adorable."

"Oh, come on," I said, feeling bashful.

"I'm serious. You're gonna be an international heartthrob after this, just wait and see."

I shook my head. "Ridiculous."

"Nope. I won't be the only one who thinks you're sexy as hell. You'll be fighting them off." He took a sip of his drink. "I mean, look at old Jimmy D."

"Who?"

"You know who I mean. James Dennis. You even got Mister Leading Himself to fall for you."

I shifted uncomfortably in my seat.

"What are you talking about?"

"Everybody on set knew the two of you had something. We watched you fall in love."

"What?" A strange mix of sensations ran through my body. My skin tingled as if all the hairs were standing on end, and my stomach felt weak as if I were suddenly seasick. "It wasn't like that."

Liberto looked at his glass with a smirk.

"Yeah, okay."

"No, really, it wasn't. I mean—I—nobody said anything about... It was just for the film. That's it."

Liberto smiled, his tongue in his cheek.

"If you say so, Zay." He laid his hand over mine, and I calmed down a little. I was making things worse, I knew it. "No judgment. It's just I've worked with the dude before and—well, I'll just say he was different this time around."

I felt a yearning that I shouldn't have felt so strongly. But I wanted him to go on talking about Dennis. All night long.

I let my fingers entwine with his.

"How was he different? I thought he got along with everybody."

"Oh, he does," agreed Liberto. "He's mad charming. Nobody ever has anything bad to say about him that I know of. But he was open this time—wide open."

"Open?"

"Look, let's just say the last time he and I worked together, I tried to get close to him. I noticed him checking me out a few times—on the low, of course. You know, straight dudes tend to like me because I blend in well. But, still, I wasn't gonna be surprised if he played it off. Except he surprised me. He didn't freak out or anything, he just told me that he didn't like to mix work with other things. With *that* kind of thing.

"Which I thought was just a polite brush-off, at first. But then I heard the same thing from a friend of mine who acted with him on another job. She's gorgeous and hilarious. But he told her the same thing. And that was before he was engaged. Long story short, he doesn't sleep around, despite his cocky, pretty boy demeanor."

I wanted to smile but I censored myself and chewed my lip instead. I moved the drink coaster in a circular motion a few times before commenting.

"But isn't that an admirable thing?"

"Sure. If you care about monogamy or whatever. But my point is, you must have been pretty special to him."

I leaned back, crossing my arms in front.

"Special? How do you figure that?"

"Dude, come on. He broke his rule for you."

I looked away. "But who said we slept together?"

Liberto chuckled and gave me serious side-eye.

"Oh, okay. So that's the game we're playing?"

He waved off the waiter and ordered two more drinks.

"I'm not playing any game," I insisted.

"Sure, *papi*," he said, clinking his glass against mine and winking. He moved closer to me in the booth and slid his hand over my thigh. "No games."

· · · ·

OUTSIDE, WE SHIVERED from the cold. I was so cold my teeth started chattering a bit, and Liberto pulled me to him, opening his coat and cocooning me inside. It was bold but he was a bold man, and it felt so good I didn't object.

"We should get out of this weather," he said and I nodded. He jerked his head to the side. "My hotel's only like ten blocks from here. You should come over if you want. I'd like for you to come over."

He wrapped his arms around me, drawing us even closer.

"Yeah, I can tell you do," I said, smiling.

Liberto leaned in and kissed me deeply. He was a great kisser, and I relished the feel of his mouth on mine. I relaxed into him, giving myself over to the feeling, and heard myself moan slightly.

"So?" he asked breathlessly. "Come?"

Just then my cell phone buzzed, twice in a row. I turned the screen to face me to swipe the notifications off, and what I saw made me pause. Two text messages from Dennis. I froze.

"It's just a yes or no, Zay," said Liberto gently. "No pressure. You don't have to wreck your emotions with every decision."

I looked up at him.

"I'm not." I pressed the cellphone against my chest and decided to ignore.

"Nah, you are—it's all over your pretty face. Every time you're struggling with something, you can read it in your expression." He lifted my chin. "It's one of the things that makes you so beautiful."

He traced his thumb along my bottom lip.

My phone buzzed again. I told myself to ignore it, but I badly wanted to check it.

Liberto smiled softly and said, "It's okay. Check it."

Maybe he really could read my expressions that well.

I glanced at the screen and saw more of the same notifications that Dennis was texting. My stomach did a flip.

"Something important?" asked Liberto. "Lemme guess—your movie star?"

I tried not to look abashed.

"No," I lied. And in that moment I knew my mind was made up. "It's my agent. I think I should probably call him back, actually. I sent in a self-tape a few days ago – for a series regular. It's a big deal, and he said he'd let me know as soon as he heard."

"Pretty late for business calls though, huh," said Liberto.

"Well, you know he's on the West Coast, and it's not that late there yet. I mean, for, like, agents..."

He smiled knowingly and nodded.

"You know, that's twice you've rejected me now, *papi*. I may start to take it personally."

I opened my mouth to protest, but he placed a finger across my lips.

He kissed me once more, this time tenderly but with meaning.

He looked at me for a second when he pulled away.

"I get it, Zay," he said. "For real, I do."

He took a couple of steps back and lifted his arms.

"I'm in town 'til Sunday. If you change your mind, you know how to find me."

"It's not that I—"

"Don't worry, baby," he interrupted. He shrugged and smiled. "Follow your heart, beautiful. But if it leads you to a dead-end, you can call me."

• • • •

I WALKED A FEW BLOCKS before looking at my phone. I felt like a complete asshole for the way I had treated Liberto, so I at least wanted to be well out of sight. I ducked inside one of the few disused phone booths that occasionally dotted the sidewalk to get out of the cutting winds.

[THE SUN-GOD]
Thanks for the birthday wishes! Hope you're good.
Sorry for the delay. In Nashville now.

Mom's been pretty sick & I'm helping out
Jae tells me the play has been going really well
You're on Broadway! How cool is that?!?!

Speaking of Jae, where was she when I needed her?! We always workshopped this type of thing. Should I text him back now? Should I wait? Then Jae's words about the cold shoulder routine came to me. *Sure, papi, no games*, Liberto had said. He was right, I had played enough games.

[ME]
It's pretty cool actually!
Sorry about your mom, I hope she's doing better.
Sending all good vibes.

I waited, my fingers flitting over the screen, flipping it back and forth. I rolled my eyes at myself, just about to toss my phone into my pocket when he wrote back.

[THE SUN-GOD]
Thanks, man! I appreciate it.
She is doing better now. We're hopeful.
Hey, did you see the new promo pix yet?

[ME]
Nooo, not yet. :(

[THE SUN-GOD]
You've gotta check them out. They're really cool.
And hot lol
I have a good feeling about this film.

[ME]
Me too. I will check them out ASAP.

[THE SUN-GOD]
Awesome!

[ME]
**I've got comps for you, any show you want
if you're in NYC any time soon.**

[THE SUN-GOD]
**Thanks, man. I would love that.
Things are hectic here so I dunno
I will try my best**

My heart sank a little.

But I'll see you on the press tour, right?

My heart buoyed.

[ME]
Most definitely!

[THE SUN-GOD]
**Better go.
Maybe we can talk later?**

[ME]
Definitely.

[THE SUN-GOD]
**Cool
[...]
[...]
[...]
I really miss you, buddy xoxo**

I felt my breath catch.

[ME]
Miss you too xx

• • • •

I BOUNDED THROUGH THE door of my studio, tore my coat off, and flopped onto my bed. I pulled up Denny's Instagram immediately. He had posted every one of the press stills and I glommed through them, feeling suddenly heartened and excited again.

Then I dug a bit deeper and found the pictures I really wanted to see—the ones I always came back to whenever I was stalking his profile—from our days in La Mancha. I had spent more time than I was prepared to admit staring at these pictures over the last few months. The one that I always dwelled on the most was the one from the church—me silhouetted against the altar, Denny watching me from behind. I loved remembering that point in time when it was all new and confusing and exciting. Knowing that he had wanted a picture of me, just the shape of me to remind him. It was like a secretive whisper between just us two.

And then there was the picture of him in the chair. How often had I stared at this? It was a snap from between shooting scenes. Denny was in a chair, on the lawn outside of the villa, lounging. He was barefoot and his shirt was open, falling away at the sides, revealing his chest. He clutched the ankle of a leg he had crossed over the other one, while his free arm hung lazily over. The breeze lifted the shorts he was wearing, making the ends billow just enough to invite a look underneath. He'd leaned back, confident, sexy, smiling broadly at the person who was taking the picture. And that person was me.

He had been staring at me.

It was a pose of seduction, and I was seduced.

After dropping my phone, I quickly shimmied out of my jeans and tore off my shirt. I zoomed in on the photo so that it took up my entire screen.

The photo I'd studied a hundred times before, my eyes tracing the curve of his lips, the line of his neck. I imagined my mouth on his chest, sucking his nipples, as I tweaked mine. On my body, I traced the path my mouth would make on his, around each nipple, down the firm, muscled torso, over the map of abs, past the waist and down, where I found my cock, erect and lying against my stomach. I lifted it and began to stroke.

At first, slowly and softly massaging, letting my foreskin ease over the head, teasing it, shuddering from the sensation. I imagined Denny's hand in place of my own, jerking my dick and whispering my name.

Oh god, I heard him say, *you're so beautiful, Zay.*

"Oh, Dennis." His name escaped my lips as a loud moan.

In my mind, the moonlight played on his skin, falling across his back, and highlighting the hard, round curve of his ass. His ass as he moved inside me, his cock as it pushed against my spot, sending shockwaves through me. I bucked my hips, thrusting my dick into my fist, staring at his half-naked body in the photo. I imagined kissing his bare feet, wrapping a hand around his powerful calf, taking his toes in my mouth and sucking on them. Tracing the inside of his thighs with my mouth, taking in the heady scent of him. Tasting his glistening skin shimmering from the heat of the day. I moaned loudly as I imagined myself worshipping his body.

"Oh, Denny," I cried out into the empty apartment, my voice full of want.

I dropped my phone and wrapped both hands around my cock. I drove myself through the shaft they created, the rough skin of my palms rasping against the sensitive head. It made me gasp, a small cry of pleasure, of pain, of sadness, of ecstasy escaped with each push.

That smooth skin, those lips in need of kissing.

I could see him in my mind, taste his mouth, the saltiness of skin, his hard hands grabbing me, pushing me about, taking me as his.

Oh, good god, Zay, I want you.

Finally, I cried out, a long moan, a clenching of my entire body as I shot ropes of pent-up frustration over the bedding and myself. I fell back onto the pillows, throwing one arm over my face, panting for breath.

When my breathing had calmed down, I rolled over, burying my face in a pillow. *How am I going to do this? I wondered. How will I survive seeing him again, every day, and not shatter into dust from the effort of resisting him?*

CHAPTER FOURTEEN

"And did you fall in love?"

"I'm sorry?" I asked, caught off guard.

"With La Mancha," clarified the moderator. "Did you fall in love with the place?"

"Oh," I said. "Most definitely."

The three of us, Carlos, Denny, and myself, were on stage after a screening of the film. It was a press event with a small audience of "civilians" as well.

"It was a magical place," I continued. "It's a place where it feels like time has almost stood still. I don't mean to suggest that the people who live there are stuck in time or not up-to-date, that's not the case at all. But the pace of life, the way in which everybody seems to luxuriate in every experience. There is no mad rush, no flying past every little detail. Things are calm there, serene, and yet everything still gets done. I think I've said this before, but it almost felt like a storybook place. Somewhere separated from the harsher aspects of life."

"And you said before that you think this experience made you a better actor?" the moderator asked, directing his question to Denny.

"I'd like to think so, yeah," he said. "I owe a lot of that to Carlos and Xavier, for inspiring me to really go for it."

"And will you be seeking out more roles like this in the future?"

"Sure," Denny said with a shrug. "Of course."

His tone wasn't curt but it was final. Nothing more to be said, it suggested. I looked over at Dennis and he met my glance with a blank expression. I averted my eyes, guilt nagging at me.

When the press junket had started, Denny was his usual ebullient self but as time went on, he had seemed to become more withdrawn, his mood increasingly cloudy. Whenever anyone mentioned that he didn't seem himself, he brought up his mother's health or claimed the repetition and tedium of the press tour were getting to him. Perfectly valid reasons, of course, but I couldn't help to think my chilly attitude had contributed.

I treated the whole experience as if it were a new project and hid behind the only defense mechanism I knew I could manage—acting. *I am playing the role of an actor,* I told myself, *an actor promoting his film.* Yet again, I was mentally trying to straddle two competing realities. But, of course, Xavier, the actor promoting his film, was not a role, it was me. And when the lights went up on a stage, or the cameras rolled in an interview, I let myself be that Xavier. That Xavier who palled around with Dennis, who told corny jokes and laughed freely, who joined in on the anecdotes of us as typical Americans who couldn't communicate with the locals. It was the Zay and Denny from last summer and the frisson was palpable to people. But as soon as the cameras went off, as soon as the lights dimmed again, my guard went back up.

The moderator turned back to me.

"I think one of the most striking things about watching this film, is the magnificent chemistry the two of you seem to have," he said. "Did that come naturally?"

"As soon as I met Dennis, I knew I'd found a brother," I answered with a short nod.

"Can you tell us a little bit more about that?" asked the moderator. "It seemed like a very intense bond the two of you had."

I leaned back in my chair, looking straight ahead. I swore I could feel Denny staring at me but I didn't dare turn my head to him.

"It was intense," I said. "We just clicked from the beginning. Of course, I was intimidated by meeting this big movie star, whom I had admired from a distance, but he put me at ease instantly. And we ended up spending a lot of time together, in prepping for the work, so our friendship became very solid in a very short amount of time. And it wasn't hard to play off of that, of course. Plus I suppose, if I'm honest, there was a little bit of hero worship on my part when we first met. It wasn't just that Dennis was a movie star, I've worked with other big names with big reputations before. But I admired him, first as a fellow actor and then as a person. How he treated everybody on the set, how he treated all the local people in the village. There was never an ounce of pretension, never an ounce of expectation on his part. He just let people be and didn't demand of them, and that impressed me."

I was caught up in my reminiscence, lost in my memory, and I leaned forward in my chair.

"Dennis just gives off good energy, you know? And I could tell that from our first encounter. Even the first day, when I showed up late and he and Carlos were standing there talking, waiting on me. There was just, like, this halo of light around him. He seemed almost otherworldly—"

I broke off then. I was suddenly hyper-aware of where I was, what I was saying. I could only imagine the tone of my voice, what people could be thinking of my words. Oh, look at the poor little gay boy, I could hear them saying, in love with the big, bad ladies' man. How precious. How sweet. How sad.

I met the moderator's eyes and he watched me, waiting. I imagined I could see the same thoughts in his eyes. I was mortified, frozen in embarrassment.

"I think that is everybody's experience on this particular film," said Carlos, interjecting. "For everyone involved this was an otherworldly experience. It was as if we had created a small little village within the village and we felt very secure and free to really explore the art of what we were doing."

Carlos delved into one of his stock answers about his creative process, and I leaned back in my seat quickly. I could feel my face flush and dipped my head, pretending to reach for my bottle of water beside my chair. Thank goodness for Carlos, I thought. If he hadn't swooped in and rescued me, god knows what kind of fool I would have made of myself. Sat there, paralyzed, my dumb mouth hanging open, shocked at my own admissions of my silly schoolboy crush. So much for my defense mechanism.

"And that was your experience as well?" the moderator asked Dennis when Carlos had finished speaking.

Dennis nodded. "Yes, the people, everybody making this film was magnificent." He paused, pursing his lips and steepling his fingers. "I think," he continued in a somber tone. "That the most special part of the experience was working with Xavier though. He's a really special person. I've never met anyone like him, in fact. Getting to know him has really made me better, in every way. If you see this film, you'll see why he's so special and why he moved me—moved us all—so much."

That was very kind of him, I thought. Very generous to mirror my compliments so that I wouldn't seem so odd and ridiculous.

I glanced at him to nod my thanks.

But what I saw cracked my heart. That cloud of sadness gathered behind his eyes, even though his face wore a smile. I gave a small nod and his smile widened ever so much.

"So, Dennis, tell us about this new project you have in the pipeline," said the moderator. "A return to your action roots, as I understand it."

Dennis turned away to answer the question and I was grateful. My throat felt parched; my eyes dry; I could barely swallow. The look in his eyes had cut right to the core of me, piercing through the façade of ice I had been so carefully cultivating.

Why did he have to be so sweet and caring and beautiful all at once? If he wasn't meant to be mine, why couldn't he just abandon me to lukewarm friendship? If I wasn't meant to have him, why couldn't he just leave me alone with the nothing I had? Me, alone, with just those few memories of sunshine and brief, ephemeral happiness.

• • • •

SHORTLY THEREAFTER awards season hit us like a ton of bricks. We were back in Spain for promos when the Oscar nominations were announced and the mood was strained. Everyone proceeded with their day, acting as if nothing were out of the ordinary. But mostly, it was a front. It was all anybody was really thinking of. I couldn't stand the waiting and posturing so just before the noms were due to be read, I went for a long walk. I asked Miranda, head of PR, to have someone text me if there was good news.

"*Four noms!!! Congrats!*" she wrote some time later before a flood of texts overwhelmed my phone.

I hurried back to the hotel. Finally, I thought, Denny would have a reason to smile. Maybe for just a moment, we would have an excuse to share a bit of genuine happiness again. Instead what I came back to was a chilled silence and most of our team gone. I found Miranda sprawled on a couch in the suite which had become our press HQ. She was fiddling with a spreadsheet on her table and looked exhausted. I asked her what was going on.

"Some didn't take the news well," she said.

"Some?"

"Yeah. Mainly Dennis."

"But why?" I asked. "Everyone's saying there were four nominations."

"There were: you, Carlos for director, the film for best film, and costume design."

"You're kidding? Nothing for Dennis?"

"Nope."

"But that's not fair. He deserves a nomination just as much as anyone else—especially as much as me."

Miranda shrugged.

"Yeah, apparently he agrees with you," she said. She waved her hand around the suite. I noticed the pile of broken wine bottles swept into a corner, the stained sofa cushion, the battered cell phone lying on a table, its face cracked.

"He had a little too much to drink and—well, truthfully, he kind of lost it."

"Denny did this? That's not like him."

"I've worked with him for a long time and it shocked the hell outta me, I gotta be honest. But it's not like he threatened or harmed anyone, other than a few innocent wine bottles. It was a bit of a hissy fit. Trust me, I've seen much worse."

"Where is he now?"

"In his room, refusing to talk to anyone. Says he's leaving in the morning. Even told Carlos to fuck off. He punched a wall earlier. Unfortunately, it was with the hand holding his cell phone. Got cut up pretty bad and I think that snapped him out of it."

I grabbed his damaged phone from the table.

"I'll talk to him."

"You sure you wanna do that, kid? He was pretty adamant. I'm sure he'll be fine in the morning."

"It's cool. I'll be okay."

She shrugged and went back to her tablet.

· · · ·

I KNOCKED TIMIDLY AT the door.

"Go away," he called out.

I knocked more insistently.

"I said fuck off!" he shouted, his voice raw.

"Denny," I said, "It's me."

The door opened a few seconds later and I followed him in. He dropped onto the bed with his back to me.

"Come to gloat?" he asked.

"Come on, man. You know that's not why I'm here, that's not me."

"So why are you here?"

"I wanted to make sure you're all right."

"Really? Cuz you've seemed to not really give a damn about me lately, except when there was a photo op involved."

"That's not true."

"It is, Zay." He turned to me, his eyes fierce. "When the cameras turn off, so do you. I know maybe I was an asshole in Spain—actually no maybe. I was. A complete asshole. I'm sorry for that; truly I am, but goddamn, man."

He broke off and turned away.

"You've just fucking iced me out completely." He rubbed his face with the bandaged hand. As if surprised by the feel of the rough material, he pulled back and stared at his hand dumbly, shaking his head. "Maybe I deserve it. I don't know. But, don't worry; I'll keep up my end. I know everybody thinks I had my diva moment, but it's over. I'll show up at all the press and praise the film and I won't take any shine from you. I would never do that anyway."

"I'm not here because I'm worried about that, Denny." He looked at me, questioning. "I came to say that it's bullshit. You shouldn't have been ignored. You're beautiful in the film."

He rolled his eyes.

"I swear if one more person calls me a fucking Ken doll."

"I'm not talking about your looks," I interjected. "I mean your performance. I've sat through more than a few screenings now. And your performance breaks my heart. Every time. You deserve some recognition. And I'm serious about that."

"Oh, I don't give a fuck about any awards," he said. "Not really. Sure, it'd be nice, but who cares. I'm fucked up because I've just been thinking, what's the fucking point of all this? These months in and out of hotels, saying the same damn thing, telling the same damn stories, over and over, again and again like some drug-addled parakeet.

"I could have been spending this time with my mom. Or doing something constructive. Doing something that made me feel alive. Yes, I'm proud of this film, damn proud of it—it's the best thing I've ever done. But that's not what kept me going. That's not what I was hoping for."

"So what were you hoping for?"

"You really don't know, do you?"

He let the question hang in the air. I looked away nervously.

"You have to know that's not the reason I'm here. I'm here for you."

"Me?"

"To repair our—whatever we had. To fix this. To make sure you don't hate me forever."

I cast my eyes down to the floor.

"I don't hate you."

"You must."

"Dennis, we've been over this. You have a fiancée—a woman who's in love with you."

"Not anymore."

I felt as if I'd been smacked across the face.

"What?"

"Ronnie and I broke up."

"When?"

"Months ago. Right after Spain. We kept it quiet; I agreed to that. Ronnie is just beginning a new phase in her career and the press, social media, they can be vicious. The truth barely matters; they'd find some way to twist the break into something ugly, something sensational. But we're just two people, not headlines. So we told everybody that matters—agents, all that, and let them control the spin. For all intents and purposes, we kept up the front—pretended like we were just the same. But we weren't—we're not. It's over."

"Because... because of us?"

"No. Yes. Partially. But mainly, because of me."

I sat heavily on the bed, feeling winded.

"It was for the best anyway, I think. I wasn't being fair to her. Or myself. We'd been distant for some time. In fact, sometimes I thought she had just agreed to marry me because she thought she could save me. Not from being who I am, I don't think she knew that, exactly. But I think she knew that something didn't completely slot into place inside me. And I think she hoped she could be the one to arrange all the pieces, make them fit. But I'm the only one who can do that, I guess."

I didn't know what to say. We sat for a long time, silently. Finally, he looked at me. He reached over and brushed a curl that had fallen in front of my eyes.

"Your hair is getting crazy long."

"Yeah, it's a mess," I replied absently.

"You changed me, Zay. Can't you see that?"

He reached for my hand, but I clasped them both together and tucked them between my thighs.

"I couldn't lie to myself anymore. And I couldn't lie to Ronnie anymore."

"Didn't you love her?" I asked.

"Of course I did. Once. I thought I did. I swore I did. Maybe I had just convinced myself because I thought I should love her. I don't know. But when I—"

"Yes?" I prompted.

"When I met you, I realized I had never been in love before. Not really—not like I felt about you."

"You don't mean that."

"I do mean that. I think I've been in love with you since that first day when you walked into that hotel lobby in La Mancha."

I shook my head. This was too much to take in.

"That must have really hurt Ronnie," I said flatly.

"It did. But eventually, she told me she was grateful that I had been honest with her, that I told her when I did. She was hurt, of course, pissed, even more so, but she said it would have been too much if I'd told her later. If we had gone through with it, the marriage. She would have ended up hating me, she said." He paused. "Like you do."

I felt a ripple of pain in my chest. "I wish I hated you, Dennis. I really do. I tried so hard to hate you but I couldn't." I stood and moved to the nearby dresser. Leaning on it, I looked at him through the mirror.

"All those months after, when I came back to New York, I couldn't get it out of my head, any of it. It, you... all of it. It was like—I don't fucking know, man—it was like I was different, as if I were changed on some level that I couldn't even comprehend. I wasn't even sure I was the same person anymore. I certainly wasn't the person I showed up as in Spain."

I turned to face him.

"And it took me all these months just to, I don't know, to get out of that haze. To feel like I knew the trajectory again. The only way I knew to stay whole was to distance myself from you, to be silent. To pretend, at least to you, that I wasn't thinking about you every damn second of every damn minute. So I can't go back to feeling like that again. Not if it's going to be the same thing in the end. I'm not sure I can survive that haze again."

He rose slowly and came over to me.

He traced the back of his hand along my cheek, ran his thumb along my bottom lip.

"Oh, Xavier," he said softly. "Do you think I haven't felt the exact same way all this time? I wish I had been better then. I wish I had given you a reason to believe in me. Won't you give me just one more chance?"

All those months of pain and yearning and need knotted inside me, begging to be set free. I met his gaze.

I could only nod.

"Thank you," he whispered and pulled me to him forcefully, kissing me hard.

Then he was on his knees; he laid his head on my stomach, wrapping his arms around me. Staring at the ceiling, I tried to staunch the feelings welling inside, threatening to overwhelm me. I willed him to stand up, walk out, leave me in my quiet misery. My hands unclenched, and I ran them through his hair. He hugged me tighter.

Looking down, I saw his eyes were closed as he rested his cheek against my skin. He must have sensed me studying him because his eyes opened, meeting mine. A storm raged in his eyes—a storm of doubt, of uncertainty, of longing, of pure need. I laid my hand on his cheek and he leaned into the caress. He lifted the hem of my shirt and kissed my stomach, his fingertips gliding gently over my skin. He cast a wanting glance up at me as he began to unbuckle my belt, pulling at my jeans.

His lips touched below my navel and moved down as his hands ran down my thighs and back up to my ass. My breath started to come in rapid little pants.

Grabbing his shoulders to still him, I then motioned for him to stand. Pulling our mouths together so that it almost hurt I kissed him, wrapping my hands around his neck. He broke off the kiss, and traced the line of my nose and then my lips. I grabbed his hand and kissed it.

"Come to bed, sweet Xavier," he whispered.

We undressed each other slowly and coiled together in our nakedness. He seemed to be enjoying the closeness, relishing the intimacy, but I felt slightly frozen. I felt petrified by the anxiety of opening up again, frightened by the depths of what I felt.

He kissed the center of my clavicle.

"Zay," he said softly. "Tonight, I want you inside me."

The newness of the request surprised me, shook me out of aloofness.

"Do you mind?" he asked.

"No. Of course not."

He pulled me to him, his tongue in my mouth, and then twisted so that we lay side by side, his leg slightly raised, offering himself to me. The thought of being inside him filled me with lust so strong I thought I might crack in two from its force.

"It's my first time... you know," he said, as I moved into position. "Be gentle."

"Always," I said.

I moved slowly, massaging his stomach and reminding him to breathe. Once I sensed he was comfortable, I slowly began to rock my hips, picking up the rhythm in accordance with his moans and gasps. Soon he was arching his back, fully opening up, his body begging for me. He reached back and pulled my head over his shoulder, bringing our mouths together.

He pushed away, flushed and panting, and moved into a new position. On his knees, he raised his haunches and lowered his head onto the sheets. I got behind and entered, running my hands down his strong, sinewy back as I thrust. I cocked one leg, angling myself as deeply as I could.

I was lost in the feel of him. And I knew I was lost. We had shared each other, given one to the other, and I knew that, no matter what came next, I could not shake this man. Be it heartbreak or eternal joy, I didn't care; I could no longer deny the want or quell the need I had for him. The taste of him, the smell of him, the feel of him, the utter madness he drove me to, it was all necessary. It might end within a season or a year or even a lifetime. Yet even if it ended in every tangible way, I would always need him, always have the want of him.

We rocked and bounced along in this cadence, breathless with passion until I heard him call out my name. His body lurched, as he threw his head back and reared. I reeled from the feeling of him grasping my body in the hold of his orgasm and I too was spent.

I lay with my head on his chest, listening to his heartbeat.

"You're not leaving, are you?" I looked up at him. "Like you told Miranda when you were upset. You're not going to leave me—leave the press tour, I mean. Are you?"

He kissed me.

"Buddy, I'm not going any damn where."

I rolled my eyes but grinned at him broadly.

"Thanks," I said. "*Buddy.*"

CHAPTER FIFTEEN

Nerves, nerves, nerves.

I swore that once everything associated with this film was done, I would need rehab at a mental hospital. Through all the drama with Denny; through this long slog of press and campaigning; finding an apartment in Los Angeles, and now finally this day. The day before the Oscars. My first major film and I was up for a major award. I was a wreck. I only hoped I could make it through the ceremony night without having a breakdown. And I hoped that if, god forbid, I actually won that I wouldn't make too much of a stuttering fool of myself during my speech.

It would be a long but thrilling evening. I desperately hoped I would see some friends there, some familiar faces. I knew Carlos and others would be there, of course, but I hadn't asked anyone to accompany me. I thought about asking my mom, and Jaelyn too. I thought she would be pissed when I told her I was thinking of going alone, but she wasn't at all. I suspected she knew the truth. The truth that I really—desperately—wanted to ask Denny. I hadn't worked up the nerve yet. I wasn't sure that he was ready to appear together in public in that intimate a pairing. People talked, especially when it came to awards shows. Apparently, the blogosphere was already thick with speculation about us. And then, too, after his nomination snub, I thought he might skip out altogether. He hadn't seemed out of sorts, but I chose not to even bring up the topic just in case.

I glanced at the time. His interview would be on shortly. He'd spent the morning at *The Midday Chat* studios recording a final press thing before the awards. I wanted to see how he talked about it all in the interview, to gauge his take better.

I had just turned on the television when he knocked at the front door.

"Oh, hey," I said, ushering him in. "I thought you had another meeting this afternoon?"

"Cancelled it," he said. He rubbed his hands together nervously. "Wanted to watch the interview with you. You remembered, right?"

"Of course I did. I just turned it on."

"Good."

He fell onto the couch and fidgeted into place.

"What's wrong?" I asked him. "I've never seen you so jumpy."

"You'll see. Come on." He waved me onto the couch.

The interview rolled along. It was the usual line, with the interviewers smiling from ear-to-ear and repeating the same stories and questions that we'd regurgitated at least a hundred times.

I glanced over at Dennis and he was watching me anxiously.

"What's up?" I asked. "I don't get it. It's just the same old tired questions they've been asking us for months."

"Shh, here it comes. Just watch, we'll talk after."

• • • •

"NOW, THERE'S BEEN A lot of talk going around," said the male interviewer on-screen. "About how this film has been an image-changer for you. Action Hero turns Sensitive Artist."

"That's true," Dennis replied.

"And a lot of people are surprised that a guy like you would take on this kind of role. Especially given this kind of material."

"This kind of material?"

"Well, the gay storyline. It still raises a lot of eyebrows for some people. Did you have any qualms about taking the role?"

"No, Bob, I honestly didn't have any qualms. The story is what is important. And the story is about love, in whatever form it takes. I think that's the most important thing."

"Would you say," interjected the co-host, "that this film changed you in any way?"

"Oh, it changed me enormously. Both professionally and personally. It gave me a new path in my career, as you said, and a new path in life as well."

"A new path?" she asked.

"Yes. One of the things I liked most about this film was the people I got to work with. I've said this before, they were all great." Here he paused and smiled thoughtfully. "I have to tell you, Bob and Yessenia, and everyone watching that one person, in particular, changed my life. My co-star, Xavier Durand. We all saw the amazing work he did on-screen, and everybody has been impressed by the grace and bearing with which he's handled this sudden new rush of attention. But it didn't surprise me one bit, either the attention or how he's handled it. I learned that he is one of the most gracious, intelligent, and beautiful, not only artists but people I've ever met."

"He certainly seems to have left an impression," agreed Yessenia.

"Oh, most definitely. And he also inspired me. To be a better artist and a better person, too. And to live my truth. You know, we developed a great friendship during and after the film, but in the last few months, it's become more. I hope he won't mind me revealing this, but we're in a relationship now, actually. I'm beyond happy. And I don't want anyone to think it's a secret or something I'm hiding. I have hidden this part of myself in the past, but he has inspired me to be braver, and to live out loud."

"Wait," said Bob. "Are you telling us that you're coming out?"

Dennis smiled and shrugged. "Yes, I suppose I am. I'm in a relationship. With a man. With Xavier."

"Well, that's quite a scoop," exclaimed Bob.

Yessenia touched Dennis's arm. "Thank you for sharing that with us. That's a beautiful thing to hear."

Dennis nodded. "Thank you."

"And," Yessenia added. "If my daughter and her friends are any indication, you just made the heads of teenage girls around the world explode. They've been shipping you two like crazy."

"Shipping?" Dennis asked, bemused.

"I'll explain during the commercial break," she said with a wink.

"Well, that was our exclusive interview with James Dennis Herbert, everybody," announced Bob to the camera. "You heard it here first on *The Midday Chat with Bob Tremont and Yessenia Lopez*. Join us after the break where we'll be making cinnamon rolls with Bubby Sherman."

• • • •

DENNIS GRABBED THE remote and flicked off the television.

The tears were rolling down my face.

"You didn't have to do that," I said.

"Of course I did. It was long overdue."

He pulled me to him and kissed me gently on the lips.

"You don't mind, do you?"

"Mind?"

"That I told everyone we're together."

"You can rent a billboard in Hollywood and blast it to the world and I wouldn't mind one bit."

"Damn," he exclaimed. "My publicist would kill for that exposure. Don't give her any ideas."

We laughed but I stopped suddenly.

"Oh. But what about your mom?"

"She knows. That trip I took to see her a few weeks ago, I told her then. I didn't tell you because I wanted to give her time. In case it was, you know, rough. But she's okay with it, actually. I know her health has improved a lot and I didn't want to get morbid, but I told her it made me realize that I couldn't stand the thought of possibly losing her at any point without her knowing the whole me. I think it shocked her, and I don't think she completely understands, but she was better than I expected. She said no matter what, she loves me and that I will always be her son. And that's something.

"But," he added with a smile, "she says she's still not going to see that dirty old film of mine. She doesn't want to see me have sex with anybody on film, man or woman."

"That's fair, I guess," I said. "It's got to be strange seeing your child doing those sorts of things. And what about Carlos?"

"I told him what I was planning yesterday. Oh, *mi amor*," he said, imitating Carlos's accent. "This is so good, the publicity! Everyone will be talking about my film now! I have made you both into gay icons!"

We laughed. He glanced at his watch and playfully punched me in the shoulder.

"We've got our final fittings in about three hours. I asked the designer to change the color of mine so that we complemented each other on-screen."

"We? So you're definitely coming to the ceremony?"

"Are you crazy? I wouldn't miss this for the world. My boyfriend's about to win an Oscar!"

"Your boyfriend, huh?"

"You got it, buddy!"

He wrapped his arms around me and kissed me. Then he lifted me up. I laughed and wrapped my legs around him, remembering that very first hug.

"Now," he declared. "That gives us plenty of time to celebrate my big announcement."

He carried me to the bedroom and lowered me onto the bed.

I looked at him, towering above me.

"Did you really mean that?"

"Oh, yes, I intend to make love to you for the rest of the afternoon."

"No," I replied, blushing and tucking a fallen curl behind my ear. "From before, do you really think I might win the Oscar?"

He laughed a deep belly laugh.

"You're fucking adorable, you know that?" He pushed me back on the bed and began kissing my neck. "And, of course, I do," he said between kisses. "You're the most amazing actor I've ever worked with. Now get undressed, movie star."

I happily complied.

COPYRIGHT

This is a work of fiction. Names, characters, places, events, and incidents are either the product of the author's imagination, used in a fictitious manner, or in public domain. Any resemblance to actual events or actual persons, living or dead, business establishments, events, or locales is coincidental.

ท

Don't miss out!

Visit the website below and you can sign up to receive emails whenever Lawrence I. Hill publishes a new book. There's no charge and no obligation.

https://books2read.com/r/B-A-LILJ-RDCDB

BOOKS 2 READ

Connecting independent readers to independent writers.

Also by Lawrence I. Hill

That Summer in Spain
Déjà Vu: A Short Romance

Watch for more at https://www.facebook.com/lawhillwrites/.

About the Author

When Lawrence was a young boy, he watched the film '84 Charing Cross Road' over and over again and dreamed of living in a grubby little studio in NYC and writing books. He's finally got the grubby little studio in the city, and now on to the rest.

Read more at https://www.facebook.com/lawhillwrites/.

MOODY BOXFAN
BOOKS

About the Publisher

Moody Boxfan Books promotes storytelling for the lesser heard voices. Life is not seen through one pair of eyes, neither should our books be.